MISS MARPLE'S FINAL CASES

ALSO BY AGATHA CHRISTIE

Mysteries
The Man in the Brown Suit
The Secret of Chimneys
The Seven Dials Mystery
The Mysterious Mr Quin
The Sittaford Mystery
The Hound of Death
The Listerdale Mystery
Why Didn't They Ask Evans?
Parker Pyne Investigates
Murder Is Easy
And Then There Were None
Towards Zero
Death Comes as the End
Sparkling Cyanide
Crooked House
They Came to Baghdad
Destination Unknown
Spider's Web *
The Unexpected Guest *
Ordeal by Innocence
The Pale Horse
Endless Night
Passenger To Frankfurt
Problem at Pollensa Bay
While the Light Lasts

Poirot
The Mysterious Affair at Styles
The Murder on the Links
Poirot Investigates
The Murder of Roger Ackroyd
The Big Four
The Mystery of the Blue Train
Black Coffee *
Peril at End House
Lord Edgware Dies
Murder on the Orient Express
Three-Act Tragedy
Death in the Clouds
The ABC Murders
Murder in Mesopotamia
Cards on the Table
Murder in the Mews
Dumb Witness
Death on the Nile
Appointment with Death
Hercule Poirot's Christmas
Sad Cypress
One, Two, Buckle My Shoe
Evil Under the Sun
Five Little Pigs
The Hollow
The Labours of Hercules
Taken at the Flood
Mrs McGinty's Dead
After the Funeral
Hickory Dickory Dock
Dead Man's Folly
Cat Among the Pigeons
The Adventure of the Christmas Pudding
The Clocks
Third Girl
Hallowe'en Party
Elephants Can Remember
Poirot's Early Cases
Curtain: Poirot's Last Case

Marple
The Murder at the Vicarage
The Thirteen Problems
The Body in the Library
The Moving Finger
A Murder Is Announced
They Do It with Mirrors
A Pocket Full of Rye
4.50 from Paddington
The Mirror Crack'd from Side to Side
A Caribbean Mystery
At Bertram's Hotel
Nemesis
Sleeping Murder
Miss Marple's Final Cases

Tommy & Tuppence
The Secret Adversary
Partners in Crime
N or M?
By the Pricking of My Thumbs
Postern of Fate

Published as Mary Westmacott
Giant's Bread
Unfinished Portrait
Absent in the Spring
The Rose and the Yew Tree
A Daughter's a Daughter
The Burden

Memoirs
An Autobiography
Come, Tell Me How You Live
The Grand Tour

Play and Stories
Akhnaton
The Mousetrap and Other Plays
The Floating Admiral †
Star Over Bethlehem
Hercule Poirot and the Greenshore Folly

* novelized by Charles Osborne † contributor

Agatha Christie®

Miss Marple's Final Cases

HarperCollins*Publishers*

HarperCollins*Publishers* Ltd
1 London Bridge Street
London SE1 9GF
www.harpercollins.co.uk

This paperback edition 2016

First published in Great Britain by
Collins, The Crime Club 1979

A catalogue record for this book is available from the British Library

ISBN 978-0-00-819664-6 (PB)
ISBN 978-0-00-825617-3 (POD PB)

Set in Sabon LT Std by Palimpsest Book Production Limited,
Falkirk, Stirlingshire

Contents

Sanctuary

The vicar's wife came round the corner of the vicarage with her arms full of chrysanthemums. A good deal of rich garden soil was attached to her strong brogue shoes and a few fragments of earth were adhering to her nose, but of that fact she was perfectly unconscious.

She had a slight struggle in opening the vicarage gate which hung, rustily, half off its hinges. A puff of wind caught at her battered felt hat, causing it to sit even more rakishly than it had done before. 'Bother!' said Bunch.

Christened by her optimistic parents Diana, Mrs Harmon had become Bunch at an early age for somewhat obvious reasons and the name had stuck to her ever since. Clutching the chrysanthemums, she made her way through the gate to the churchyard, and so to the church door.

The November air was mild and damp. Clouds scudded across the sky with patches of blue here and there. Inside, the church was dark and cold; it was unheated except at service times.

'Brrrrrh!' said Bunch expressively. 'I'd better get on with this quickly. I don't want to die of cold.'

With the quickness born of practice she collected the necessary paraphernalia: vases, water, flower-holders. 'I wish we had lilies,' thought Bunch to herself. 'I get so tired of these scraggy chrysanthemums.' Her nimble fingers arranged the blooms in their holders.

There was nothing particularly original or artistic about the decorations, for Bunch Harmon herself was neither original nor artistic, but it was a homely and pleasant arrangement. Carrying the vases carefully, Bunch stepped up the aisle and made her way towards the altar. As she did so the sun came out.

It shone through the east window of somewhat crude coloured glass, mostly blue and red—the gift of a wealthy Victorian churchgoer. The effect was almost startling in its sudden opulence. 'Like jewels,' thought Bunch. Suddenly she stopped, staring ahead of her. On the chancel steps was a huddled dark form.

Putting down the flowers carefully, Bunch went up to it and bent over it. It was a man lying there, huddled over on himself. Bunch knelt down by him and slowly, carefully, she turned him over. Her fingers went to his pulse—a pulse so feeble and fluttering that it told its own story, as did the almost greenish pallor of his face. There was no doubt, Bunch thought, that the man was dying.

He was a man of about forty-five, dressed in a dark, shabby suit. She laid down the limp hand she had picked up and looked at his other hand. This seemed clenched like a fist on his breast. Looking more closely she saw that the fingers were closed over what seemed to be a large wad or handkerchief which he was holding tightly to his chest. All round the clenched hand there were splashes of a dry brown fluid which, Bunch guessed, was dry blood. Bunch sat back on her heels, frowning.

Up till now the man's eyes had been closed but at this point they suddenly opened and fixed themselves on Bunch's face. They were neither dazed nor wandering. They seemed fully alive and intelligent. His lips moved, and Bunch bent forward to catch the words, or rather the word. It was only one word that he said:

'Sanctuary.'

There was, she thought, just a very faint smile as he breathed out this word. There was no mistaking it, for after a moment he said it again, 'Sanctuary . . .'

Then, with a faint, long-drawn-out sigh, his eyes closed again. Once more Bunch's fingers went to his pulse. It was still there, but fainter now and more intermittent. She got up with decision.

'Don't move,' she said, 'or try to move. I'm going for help.'

The man's eyes opened again but he seemed now to be fixing his attention on the coloured light that came through the east window. He murmured something that Bunch could not quite catch. She thought, startled, that it might have been her husband's name.

'Julian?' she said. 'Did you come here to find Julian?' But there was no answer. The man lay with eyes closed, his breathing coming in slow, shallow fashion.

Bunch turned and left the church rapidly. She glanced at her watch and nodded with some satisfaction. Dr Griffiths would still be in his surgery. It was only a couple of minutes' walk from the church. She went in, without waiting to knock or ring, passing through the waiting room and into the doctor's surgery.

'You must come at once,' said Bunch. 'There's a man dying in the church.'

Some minutes later Dr Griffiths rose from his knees after a brief examination.

'Can we move him from here into the vicarage? I can attend to him better there—not that it's any use.'

'Of course,' said Bunch. 'I'll go along and get things ready. I'll get Harper and Jones, shall I? To help you carry him.'

'Thanks. I can telephone from the vicarage for an ambulance, but I'm afraid—by the time it comes . . .' He left the remark unfinished.

Bunch said, 'Internal bleeding?'

Dr Griffiths nodded. He said, 'How on earth did he come here?'

'I think he must have been here all night,' said Bunch, considering. 'Harper unlocks the church in the morning as he goes to work, but he doesn't usually come in.'

It was about five minutes later when Dr Griffiths put down the telephone receiver and came back into the morning-room where the injured man was lying on quickly arranged blankets on the sofa. Bunch was moving a basin of water and clearing up after the doctor's examination.

'Well, that's that,' said Griffiths. 'I've sent for an ambulance and I've notified the police.' He stood, frowning, looking down on the patient who lay with closed eyes. His left hand was plucking in a nervous, spasmodic way at his side.

'He was shot,' said Griffiths. 'Shot at fairly close quarters. He rolled his handkerchief up into a ball and plugged the wound with it so as to stop the bleeding.'

'Could he have gone far after that happened?' Bunch asked.

'Oh, yes, it's quite possible. A mortally wounded man has been known to pick himself up and walk along a street as though nothing had happened, and then suddenly collapse five or ten minutes later. So he needn't have been shot in the church. Oh no. He may have been shot some distance away. Of course, he may have shot himself and then dropped the revolver and staggered blindly towards the church. I don't quite know why he made for the church and not for the vicarage.'

'Oh, I know *that*,' said Bunch. 'He said it: "Sanctuary."'

The doctor stared at her. 'Sanctuary?'

'Here's Julian,' said Bunch, turning her head as she heard her husband's steps in the hall. 'Julian! Come here.'

The Reverend Julian Harmon entered the room. His vague, scholarly manner always made him appear much older than he really was. 'Dear me!' said Julian Harmon, staring in a mild, puzzled manner at the surgical appliances and the prone figure on the sofa.

Bunch explained with her usual economy of words. 'He was in the church, dying. He'd been shot. Do you know him, Julian? I thought he said your name.'

The vicar came up to the sofa and looked down at the dying man. 'Poor fellow,' he said, and shook his head. 'No, I don't know him. I'm almost sure I've never seen him before.'

At that moment the dying man's eyes opened once more. They went from the doctor to Julian Harmon and from him to his wife. The eyes stayed there, staring into Bunch's face. Griffiths stepped forward.

'If you could tell us,' he said urgently.

But with his eyes fixed on Bunch, the man said in a weak voice, 'Please—*please*—' And then, with a slight tremor, he died . . .

Sergeant Hayes licked his pencil and turned the page of his notebook.

'So that's all you can tell me, Mrs Harmon?'

'That's all,' said Bunch. 'These are the things out of his coat pockets.'

On a table at Sergeant Hayes's elbow was a wallet, a rather battered old watch with the initials W.S. and the return half of a ticket to London. Nothing more.

'You've found out who he is?' asked Bunch.

'A Mr and Mrs Eccles phoned up the station. He's her brother, it seems. Name of Sandbourne. Been in a low state of health and nerves for some time. He's been getting worse lately. The day before yesterday he walked out and didn't come back. He took a revolver with him.'

'And he came out here and shot himself with it?' said Bunch. 'Why?'

'Well, you see, he'd been depressed . . .'

Bunch interrupted him. 'I don't mean *that*. I mean, why here?'

Since Sergeant Hayes obviously did not know the answer to that one, he replied in an oblique fashion, 'Come out here, he did, on the five-ten bus.'

'Yes,' said Bunch again. 'But *why*?'

'I don't know, Mrs Harmon,' said Sergeant Hayes. 'There's no accounting. If the balance of the mind is disturbed—'

Bunch finished for him. 'They may do it anywhere. But it still seems to me unnecessary to take a bus out to a small country place like this. He didn't know anyone here, did he?'

'Not so far as can be ascertained,' said Sergeant Hayes. He coughed in an apologetic manner and said, as he rose to his feet, 'It may be as Mr and Mrs Eccles will come out and see you, ma'am—if you don't mind, that is.'

'Of course I don't mind,' said Bunch. 'It's very natural. I only wish I had something to tell them.'

'I'll be getting along,' said Sergeant Hayes.

'I'm only so thankful,' said Bunch, going with him to the front door, 'that it wasn't murder.'

A car had driven up at the vicarage gate. Sergeant Hayes, glancing at it, remarked: 'Looks as though that's Mr and Mrs Eccles come here now, ma'am, to talk with you.'

Bunch braced herself to endure what, she felt, might be rather a difficult ordeal. 'However,' she thought, 'I can always call Julian to help me. A clergyman's a great help when people are bereaved.'

Exactly what she had expected Mr and Mrs Eccles to be like, Bunch could not have said, but she was conscious, as she greeted them, of a feeling of surprise. Mr Eccles was a stout florid man whose natural manner would have been cheerful and facetious. Mrs Eccles had a vaguely flashy look about her. She had a small, mean, pursed-up mouth. Her voice was thin and reedy.

'It's been a terrible shock, Mrs Harmon, as you can imagine,' she said.

'Oh, I know,' said Bunch. 'It must have been. Do sit down. Can I offer you—well, perhaps it's a little early for tea—'

Mr Eccles waved a pudgy hand. 'No, no, nothing for us,' he said. 'It's very kind of you, I'm sure. Just wanted to . . . well . . . what poor William said and all that, you know?'

'He's been abroad a long time,' said Mrs Eccles, 'and I think he must have had some very nasty experiences. Very quiet and depressed he's been, ever since he came home. Said the world wasn't fit to live in and there was nothing to look forward to. Poor Bill, he was always moody.'

Bunch stared at them both for a moment or two without speaking.

'Pinched my husband's revolver, he did,' went on Mrs Eccles. 'Without our knowing. Then it seems he come here by bus. I suppose that was nice feeling on his part. He wouldn't have liked to do it in our house.'

'Poor fellow, poor fellow,' said Mr Eccles, with a sigh. 'It doesn't do to judge.'

There was another short pause, and Mr Eccles said, 'Did he leave a message? Any last words, nothing like that?'

His bright, rather pig-like eyes watched Bunch closely. Mrs Eccles, too, leaned forward as though anxious for the reply.

'No,' said Bunch quietly. 'He came into the church when he was dying, for sanctuary.'

Mrs Eccles said in a puzzled voice. 'Sanctuary? I don't think I quite . . .'

Mr Eccles interrupted. 'Holy place, my dear,' he said impatiently. 'That's what the vicar's wife means. It's a sin—suicide, you know. I expect he wanted to make amends.'

'He tried to say something just before he died,' said Bunch. 'He began, "Please," but that's as far as he got.'

Mrs Eccles put her handkerchief to her eyes and sniffed. 'Oh, dear,' she said. 'It's terribly upsetting, isn't it?'

'There, there, Pam,' said her husband. 'Don't take on. These things can't be helped. Poor Willie. Still, he's at peace now. Well, thank you very much, Mrs Harmon. I hope we haven't interrupted you. A vicar's wife is a busy lady, we know that.'

They shook hands with her. Then Eccles turned back suddenly to say, 'Oh yes, there's just one other thing. I think you've got his coat here, haven't you?'

'His coat?' Bunch frowned.

Mrs Eccles said, 'We'd like all his things, you know. Sentimental-like.'

'He had a watch and a wallet and a railway ticket in the pockets,' said Bunch. 'I gave them to Sergeant Hayes.'

'That's all right, then,' said Mr Eccles. 'He'll hand them over to us, I expect. His private papers would be in the wallet.'

'There was a pound note in the wallet,' said Bunch. 'Nothing else.'

'No letters? Nothing like that?'

Bunch shook her head.

'Well, thank you again, Mrs Harmon. The coat he was wearing—perhaps the sergeant's got that too, has he?'

Bunch frowned in an effort of remembrance.

'No,' she said. 'I don't think . . . let me see. The doctor and I took his coat off to examine his wound.' She looked round the room vaguely. 'I must have taken it upstairs with the towels and basin.'

'I wonder now, Mrs Harmon, if you don't mind . . . We'd like his coat, you know, the last thing he wore. Well, the wife feels rather sentimental about it.'

'Of course,' said Bunch. 'Would you like me to have it cleaned first? I'm afraid it's rather—well—stained.'

'Oh, no, no, no, that doesn't matter.'

Bunch frowned. 'Now I wonder where . . . excuse me a moment.' She went upstairs and it was some few minutes before she returned.

'I'm so sorry,' she said breathlessly, 'my daily woman must have put it aside with other clothes that were going to the cleaners. It's taken me quite a long time to find it. Here it is. I'll do it up for you in brown paper.'

Disclaiming their protests she did so; then once more effusively bidding her farewell the Eccleses departed.

Bunch went slowly back across the hall and entered the study. The Reverend Julian Harmon looked up and his brow cleared. He was composing a sermon and was fearing that he'd been led astray by the interest of the political relations between Judaea and Persia, in the reign of Cyrus.

'Yes, dear?' he said hopefully.

'Julian,' said Bunch. 'What's *Sanctuary* exactly?'

Julian Harmon gratefully put aside his sermon paper.

'Well,' he said. 'Sanctuary in Roman and Greek temples applied to the *cella* in which stood the statue of a god. The Latin word for altar "*ara*" also means protection.' He continued learnedly: 'In three hundred and ninety-nine A.D. the right of sanctuary in Christian churches was finally and definitely recognized. The earliest mention of the right of sanctuary in England is in the Code of Laws issued by Ethelbert in A.D. six hundred . . .'

He continued for some time with his exposition but was, as often, disconcerted by his wife's reception of his erudite pronouncement.

'Darling,' she said. 'You *are* sweet.'

Bending over, she kissed him on the tip of his nose. Julian felt rather like a dog who has been congratulated on performing a clever trick.

'The Eccleses have been here,' said Bunch.

The vicar frowned. 'The Eccleses? I don't seem to remember . . .'

'You don't know them. They're the sister and her husband of the man in the church.'

'My dear, you ought to have called me.'

'There wasn't any need,' said Bunch. 'They were not in need of consolation. I wonder now . . .' She frowned. 'If I put a casserole in the oven tomorrow, can you manage, Julian? I think I shall go up to London for the sales.'

'The sails?' Her husband looked at her blankly. 'Do you mean a yacht or a boat or something?'

Bunch laughed. 'No, darling. There's a special white sale at Burrows and Portman's. You know, sheets, table cloths and towels and glass-cloths. I don't know what we do with our glass-cloths, the way they wear through. Besides,' she added thoughtfully, 'I think I ought to go and see Aunt Jane.'

That sweet old lady, Miss Jane Marple, was enjoying the delights of the metropolis for a fortnight, comfortably installed in her nephew's studio flat.

'So kind of dear Raymond,' she murmured. 'He and Joan have gone to America for a fortnight and they insisted I should come up here and enjoy myself. And now, dear Bunch, do tell me what it is that's worrying you.'

Bunch was Miss Marple's favourite godchild, and the old lady looked at her with great affection as Bunch, thrusting her best felt hat farther on the back of her head, started her story.

Bunch's recital was concise and clear. Miss Marple nodded her head as Bunch finished. 'I see,' she said. 'Yes, I see.'

'That's why I felt I had to see you,' said Bunch. 'You see, not being clever—'

'But you *are* clever, my dear.'

'No, I'm not. Not clever like Julian.'

'Julian, of course, has a very solid intellect,' said Miss Marple.

'That's it,' said Bunch. 'Julian's got the intellect, but on the other hand, I've got the *sense*.'

'You have a lot of common sense, Bunch, and you're very intelligent.'

'You see, I don't really know what I ought to do. I can't

ask Julian because—well, I mean, Julian's so full of rectitude . . .'

This statement appeared to be perfectly understood by Miss Marple, who said, 'I know what you mean, dear. We women—well, it's different.' She went on. 'You told me what happened, Bunch, but I'd like to know first exactly what you think.'

'It's all wrong,' said Bunch. 'The man who was there in the church, dying, knew all about Sanctuary. He said it just the way Julian would have said it. I mean, he was a well-read, educated man. And if he'd shot himself, he wouldn't drag himself to a church afterwards and say "sanctuary". Sanctuary means that you're pursued, and when you get into a church you're safe. Your pursuers can't touch you. At one time even the law couldn't get at you.'

She looked questioningly at Miss Marple. The latter nodded. Bunch went on, 'Those people, the Eccleses, were quite different. Ignorant and coarse. And there's another thing. That watch—the dead man's watch. It had the initials W.S. on the back of it. But inside—I opened it—in very small lettering there was "To Walter from his father" and a date. *Walter*. But the Eccleses kept talking of him as William or Bill.'

Miss Marple seemed about to speak but Bunch rushed on. 'Oh, I know you're not always called the name you're baptized by. I mean, I can understand that you might be christened William and called "Porgy" or "Carrots" or something. But your sister wouldn't call you William or Bill if your name was Walter.'

'You mean that she wasn't his sister?'

'I'm quite sure she wasn't his sister. They were horrid—both of them. They came to the vicarage to get his things and to find out if he'd said anything before he died. When I said he hadn't I saw it in their faces—relief. I think myself,' finished Bunch, 'it was Eccles who shot him.'

'Murder?' said Miss Marple.

'Yes,' said Bunch. 'Murder. That's why I came to you, darling.'

Bunch's remark might have seemed incongruous to an ignorant listener, but in certain spheres Miss Marple had a reputation for dealing with murder.

'He said "please" to me before he died,' said Bunch. 'He wanted me to do something for him. The awful thing is I've no idea what.'

Miss Marple considered for a moment or two, and then pounced on the point that had already occurred to Bunch. 'But why was he there at all?' she asked.

'You mean,' said Bunch, 'if you wanted sanctuary you might pop into a church anywhere. There's no need to take a bus that only goes four times a day and come out to a lonely spot like ours for it.'

'He must have come there for a purpose,' Miss Marple thought. 'He must have come to see someone. Chipping Cleghorn's not a big place, Bunch. Surely you must have some idea of who it was he came to see?'

Bunch reviewed the inhabitants of her village in her mind before rather doubtfully shaking her head. 'In a way,' she said, 'it could be anybody.'

'He never mentioned a name?'

'He said Julian, or I thought he said Julian. It might

have been Julia, I suppose. As far as I know, there isn't any Julia living in Chipping Cleghorn.'

She screwed up her eyes as she thought back to the scene. The man lying there on the chancel steps, the light coming through the window with its jewels of red and blue light.

'Jewels,' said Bunch suddenly. 'Perhaps that's what he said. The light coming through the east window looked like jewels.'

'Jewels,' said Miss Marple thoughtfully.

'I'm coming now,' said Bunch, 'to the most important thing of all. The reason why I've really come here today. You see, the Eccleses made a great fuss about having his coat. We took it off when the doctor was seeing him. It was an old, shabby sort of coat—there was no reason they should have wanted it. They pretended it was sentimental, but that was nonsense.

'Anyway, I went up to find it, and as I was just going up the stairs I remembered how he'd made a kind of picking gesture with his hand, as though he was fumbling with the coat. So when I got hold of the coat I looked at it very carefully and I saw that in one place the lining had been sewn up again with a different thread. So I unpicked it and I found a little piece of paper inside. I took it out and I sewed it up again properly with thread that matched. I was careful and I don't really think that the Eccleses would know I've done it. I don't *think* so, but I can't be sure. And I took the coat down to them and made some excuse for the delay.'

'The piece of paper?' asked Miss Marple.

Bunch opened her handbag. 'I didn't show it to Julian,' she said, 'because he would have said that I ought to have given it to the Eccleses. But I thought I'd rather bring it to you instead.'

'A cloakroom ticket,' said Miss Marple, looking at it. 'Paddington Station.'

'He had a return ticket to Paddington in his pocket,' said Bunch.

The eyes of the two women met.

'This calls for action,' said Miss Marple briskly. 'But it would be advisable, I think, to be careful. Would you have noticed at all, Bunch dear, whether you were followed when you came to London today?'

'Followed!' exclaimed Bunch. 'You don't think—'

'Well, I think it's *possible*,' said Miss Marple. 'When anything is possible, I think we ought to take precautions.' She rose with a brisk movement. 'You came up here ostensibly, my dear, to go to the sales. I think the right thing to do, therefore, would be for us to *go* to the sales. But before we set out, we might put one or two little arrangements in hand. I don't suppose,' Miss Marple added obscurely, 'that I shall need the old speckled tweed with the beaver collar just at present.'

It was about an hour and a half later that the two ladies, rather the worse for wear and battered in appearance, and both clasping parcels of hardly-won household linen, sat down at a small and sequestered hostelry called the Apple Bough to restore their forces with steak and kidney pudding followed by apple tart and custard.

'Really a prewar quality face towel,' gasped Miss Marple, slightly out of breath. 'With a J on it, too. So fortunate that Raymond's wife's name is Joan. I shall put them aside until I really need them and then they will do for her if I pass on sooner than I expect.'

'I really did need the glass-cloths,' said Bunch. 'And they were very cheap, though not as cheap as the ones that woman with the ginger hair managed to snatch from me.'

A smart young woman with a lavish application of rouge and lipstick entered the Apple Bough at that moment. After looking around vaguely for a moment or two, she hurried to their table. She laid down an envelope by Miss Marple's elbow.

'There you are, miss,' she said briskly.

'Oh, thank you, Gladys,' said Miss Marple. 'Thank you very much. So kind of you.'

'Always pleased to oblige, I'm sure,' said Gladys. 'Ernie always says to me, "Everything what's good you learned from that Miss Marple of yours that you were in service with," and I'm sure I'm always glad to oblige you, miss.'

'Such a dear girl,' said Miss Marple as Gladys departed again. 'Always so willing and so kind.'

She looked inside the envelope and then passed it on to Bunch. 'Now be very careful, dear,' she said. 'By the way, is there still that nice young inspector at Melchester that I remember?'

'I don't know,' said Bunch. 'I expect so.'

'Well, if not,' said Miss Marple thoughtfully. 'I can always ring up the Chief Constable. I *think* he would remember me.'

'Of course he'd remember you,' said Bunch. 'Everybody would remember *you*. You're quite unique.' She rose.

Arrived at Paddington, Bunch went to the luggage office and produced the cloakroom ticket. A moment or two later a rather shabby old suitcase was passed across to her, and carrying this she made her way to the platform.

The journey home was uneventful. Bunch rose as the train approached Chipping Cleghorn and picked up the old suitcase. She had just left her carriage when a man, sprinting along the platform, suddenly seized the suitcase from her hand and rushed off with it.

'Stop!' Bunch yelled. 'Stop him, stop him. He's taken my suitcase.'

The ticket collector who, at this rural station, was a man of somewhat slow processes, had just begun to say, 'Now, look here, you can't do that—' when a smart blow on the chest pushed him aside, and the man with the suitcase rushed out from the station. He made his way towards a waiting car. Tossing the suitcase in, he was about to climb after it, but before he could move a hand fell on his shoulder, and the voice of Police Constable Abel said, 'Now then, what's all this?'

Bunch arrived, panting, from the station. 'He snatched my suitcase,' she said.

'Nonsense,' said the man. 'I don't know what this lady means. It's my suitcase. I just got out of the train with it.'

'Now, let's get this clear,' said Police Constable Abel.

He looked at Bunch with a bovine and impartial stare. Nobody would have guessed that Police Constable Abel and Mrs Harmon spent long half-hours in Police Constable Abel's off-time discussing the respective merits of manure and bone meal for rose bushes.

'You say, madam, that this is your suitcase?' said Police Constable Abel.

'Yes,' said Bunch. 'Definitely.'

'And you, sir?'

'I say this suitcase is mine.'

The man was tall, dark and well dressed, with a drawling voice and a superior manner. A feminine voice from inside the car said, 'Of course it's your suitcase, Edwin. I don't know what this woman means.'

'We'll have to get this clear,' said Police Constable Abel. 'If it's your suitcase, madam, what do you say is inside it?'

'Clothes,' said Bunch. 'A long speckled coat with a beaver collar, two wool jumpers and a pair of shoes.'

'Well, that's clear enough,' said Police Constable Abel. He turned to the other.

'I am a theatrical costumer,' said the dark man importantly. 'This suitcase contains theatrical properties which I brought down here for an amateur performance.'

'Right, sir,' said Police Constable Abel. 'Well, we'll just look inside, shall we, and see? We can go along to the police station, or if you're in a hurry we'll take the suitcase back to the station and open it there.'

'It'll suit me,' said the dark man. 'My name is Moss, by the way, Edwin Moss.'

The police constable, holding the suitcase, went back into the station. 'Just taking this into the parcels office, George,' he said to the ticket collector.

Police Constable Abel laid the suitcase on the counter of the parcels office and pushed back the clasp. The case was not locked. Bunch and Mr Edwin Moss stood on either side of him, their eyes regarding each other vengefully.

'Ah!' said Police Constable Abel, as he pushed up the lid.

Inside, neatly folded, was a long rather shabby tweed coat with a beaver fur collar. There were also two wool jumpers and a pair of country shoes.

'Exactly as you say, madam,' said Police Constable Abel, turning to Bunch.

Nobody could have said that Mr Edwin Moss underdid things. His dismay and compunction were magnificent.

'I do apologize,' he said. 'I really *do* apologize. Please believe me, dear lady, when I tell you how very, very sorry I am. Unpardonable—quite unpardonable—my behaviour has been.' He looked at his watch. 'I must rush now. Probably my suitcase has gone on the train.' Raising his hat once more, he said meltingly to Bunch, 'Do, *do* forgive me,' and rushed hurriedly out of the parcels office.

'Are you going to let him get away?' asked Bunch in a conspiratorial whisper to Police Constable Abel.

The latter slowly closed a bovine eye in a wink.

'He won't get too far, ma'am,' he said. 'That's to say he won't get far unobserved, if you take my meaning.'

'Oh,' said Bunch, relieved.

'That old lady's been on the phone,' said Police Constable Abel, 'the one as was down here a few years ago. Bright she is, isn't she? But there's been a lot cooking up all today. Shouldn't wonder if the inspector or sergeant was out to see you about it tomorrow morning.'

It was the inspector who came, the Inspector Craddock whom Miss Marple remembered. He greeted Bunch with a smile as an old friend.

'Crime in Chipping Cleghorn again,' he said cheerfully. 'You don't lack for sensation here, do you, Mrs Harmon?'

'I could do with rather less,' said Bunch. 'Have you come to ask me questions or are you going to tell me things for a change?'

'I'll tell you some things first,' said the inspector. 'To begin with, Mr and Mrs Eccles have been having an eye kept on them for some time. There's reason to believe they've been connected with several robberies in this part of the world. For another thing, although Mrs Eccles *has* a brother called Sandbourne who has recently come back from abroad, the man you found dying in the church yesterday was definitely not Sandbourne.'

'I knew that he wasn't,' said Bunch. 'His name was Walter, to begin with, not William.'

The inspector nodded. 'His name was Walter St John, and he escaped forty-eight hours ago from Charrington Prison.'

'Of course,' said Bunch softly to herself, 'he was being hunted down by the law, and he took sanctuary.' Then she asked, 'What had he done?'

'I'll have to go back rather a long way. It's a complicated story. Several years ago there was a certain dancer doing turns at the music halls. I don't expect you'll have ever heard of her, but she specialized in an Arabian Night turn, "Aladdin in the Cave of Jewels" it was called. She wore bits of rhinestone and not much else.

'She wasn't much of a dancer, I believe, but she was—well—attractive. Anyway, a certain Asiatic royalty fell for her in a big way. Amongst other things he gave her a very magnificent emerald necklace.'

'The historic jewels of a Rajah?' murmured Bunch ecstatically.

Inspector Craddock coughed. 'Well, a rather more modern version, Mrs Harmon. The affair didn't last very long, broke up when our potentate's attention was captured by a certain film star whose demands were not quite so modest.

'Zobeida, to give the dancer her stage name, hung on to the necklace, and in due course it was stolen. It disappeared from her dressing-room at the theatre, and there was a lingering suspicion in the minds of the authorities that she herself might have engineered its disappearance. Such things have been known as a publicity stunt, or indeed from more dishonest motives.

'The necklace was never recovered, but during the course of the investigation the attention of the police was drawn to this man, Walter St John. He was a man of education and breeding who had come down in the world, and who was employed as a working jeweller with a rather obscure firm which was suspected of acting as a fence for jewel robberies.

'There was evidence that this necklace had passed through his hands. It was, however, in connection with the theft of some other jewellery that he was finally brought to trial and convicted and sent to prison. He had not very much longer to serve, so his escape was rather a surprise.'

'But why did he come here?' asked Bunch.

'We'd like to know that very much, Mrs Harmon. Following up his trial, it seems that he went first to London. He didn't visit any of his old associates but he visited an elderly woman, a Mrs Jacobs who had formerly been a theatrical dresser. She won't say a word of what he came for, but according to other lodgers in the house he left carrying a suitcase.'

'I see,' said Bunch. 'He left it in the cloakroom at Paddington and then he came down here.'

'By that time,' said Inspector Craddock, 'Eccles and the man who calls himself Edwin Moss were on his trail. They wanted that suitcase. They saw him get on the bus. They must have driven out in a car ahead of him and been waiting for him when he left the bus.'

'And he was murdered?' said Bunch.

'Yes,' said Craddock. 'He was shot. It was Eccles's revolver, but I rather fancy it was Moss who did the shooting. Now, Mrs Harmon, what we want to know is, where is the suitcase that Walter St John actually deposited at Paddington Station?'

Bunch grinned. 'I expect Aunt Jane's got it by now,' she said. 'Miss Marple, I mean. That was her plan. She sent a former maid of hers with a suitcase packed with her things to the cloakroom at Paddington and we exchanged tickets. I collected her suitcase and brought it down by train. She seemed to expect that an attempt would be made to get it from me.'

It was Inspector Craddock's turn to grin. 'So she said when she rang up. I'm driving up to London to see her. Do you want to come, too, Mrs Harmon?'

'Wel-l,' said Bunch, considering. 'Wel-l, as a matter of fact, it's very fortunate. I had a toothache last night so I really ought to go to London to see the dentist, oughtn't I?'

'Definitely,' said Inspector Craddock . . .

Miss Marple looked from Inspector Craddock's face to

the eager face of Bunch Harmon. The suitcase lay on the table. 'Of course, I haven't opened it,' the old lady said. 'I wouldn't dream of doing such a thing till somebody official arrived. Besides,' she added, with a demurely mischievous Victorian smile, 'it's locked.'

'Like to make a guess at what's inside, Miss Marple?' asked the inspector.

'I should imagine, you know,' said Miss Marple, 'that it would be Zobeida's theatrical costumes. Would you like a chisel, Inspector?'

The chisel soon did its work. Both women gave a slight gasp as the lid flew up. The sunlight coming through the window lit up what seemed like an inexhaustible treasure of sparkling jewels, red, blue, green, orange.

'Aladdin's Cave,' said Miss Marple. 'The flashing jewels the girl wore to dance.'

'Ah,' said Inspector Craddock. 'Now, what's so precious about it, do you think, that a man was murdered to get hold of it?'

'She was a shrewd girl, I expect,' said Miss Marple thoughtfully. 'She's dead, isn't she, Inspector?'

'Yes, died three years ago.'

'She had this valuable emerald necklace,' said Miss Marple, musingly. 'Had the stones taken out of their setting and fastened here and there on her theatrical costume, where everyone would take them for merely coloured rhinestones. Then she had a replica made of the real necklace, and that, of course, was what was stolen. No wonder it never came on the market. The thief soon discovered the stones were false.'

'Here is an envelope,' said Bunch, pulling aside some of the glittering stones.

Inspector Craddock took it from her and extracted two official-looking papers from it. He read aloud, '"Marriage Certificate between Walter Edmund St John and Mary Moss." That was Zobeida's real name.'

'So they were married,' said Miss Marple. 'I see.'

'What's the other?' asked Bunch.

'A birth certificate of a daughter, Jewel.'

'Jewel?' cried Bunch. 'Why, of course. Jewel! *Jill!* That's it. I see now why he came to Chipping Cleghorn. *That's* what he was trying to say to me. Jewel. The Mundys, you know. Laburnum Cottage. They look after a little girl for someone. They're devoted to her. She's been like their own granddaughter. Yes, I remember now, her name *was* Jewel, only, of course, they call her Jill.

'Mrs Mundy had a stroke about a week ago, and the old man's been very ill with pneumonia. They were both going to go to the infirmary. I've been trying hard to find a good home for Jill somewhere. I didn't want her taken away to an institution.

'I suppose her father heard about it in prison and he managed to break away and get hold of this suitcase from the old dresser he or his wife left it with. I suppose if the jewels really belonged to her mother, they can be used for the child now.'

'I should imagine so, Mrs Harmon. *If* they're here.'

'Oh, they'll be here all right,' said Miss Marple cheerfully . . .

*

'Thank goodness you're back, dear,' said the Reverend Julian Harmon, greeting his wife with affection and a sigh of content. 'Mrs Burt always tries to do her best when you're away, but she really gave me some *very* peculiar fish-cakes for lunch. I didn't want to hurt her feelings so I gave them to Tiglath Pileser, but even *he* wouldn't eat them so I had to throw them out of the window.'

'Tiglath Pileser,' said Bunch, stroking the vicarage cat, who was purring against her knee, 'is *very* particular about what fish he eats. I often tell him he's got a proud stomach!'

'And your tooth, dear? Did you have it seen to?'

'Yes,' said Bunch. 'It didn't hurt much, and I went to see Aunt Jane again, too . . .'

'Dear old thing,' said Julian. 'I hope she's not failing at all.'

'Not in the least,' said Bunch, with a grin.

The following morning Bunch took a fresh supply of chrysanthemums to the church. The sun was once more pouring through the east window, and Bunch stood in the jewelled light on the chancel steps. She said very softly under her breath, 'Your little girl will be all right. *I'll* see that she is. I promise.'

Then she tidied up the church, slipped into a pew and knelt for a few moments to say her prayers before returning to the vicarage to attack the piled-up chores of two neglected days.

Strange Jest

'And this,' said Jane Helier, completing her introductions, 'is Miss Marple!'

Being an actress, she was able to make her point. It was clearly the climax, the triumphant finale! Her tone was equally compounded of reverent awe and triumph.

The odd part of it was that the object thus proudly proclaimed was merely a gentle, fussy-looking, elderly spinster. In the eyes of the two young people who had just, by Jane's good offices, made her acquaintance, there showed incredulity and a tinge of dismay. They were nice-looking people; the girl, Charmian Stroud, slim and dark—the man, Edward Rossiter, a fair-haired, amiable young giant.

Charmian said a little breathlessly. 'Oh! We're awfully pleased to meet you.' But there was doubt in her eyes. She flung a quick, questioning glance at Jane Helier.

'Darling,' said Jane, answering the glance, 'she's absolutely *marvellous*. Leave it all to her. I told you I'd get her here and I have.' She added to Miss Marple, '*You'll* fix it for them, I know. It will be easy for *you*.'

Miss Marple turned her placid, china-blue eyes towards

Mr Rossiter. 'Won't you tell me,' she said, 'what all this is about?'

'Jane's a friend of ours,' Charmian broke in impatiently. 'Edward and I are in rather a fix. Jane said if we would come to her party, she'd introduce us to someone who was—who would—who could—'

Edward came to the rescue. 'Jane tells us you're the last word in sleuths, Miss Marple!'

The old lady's eyes twinkled, but she protested modestly. 'Oh, no, no! Nothing of the kind. It's just that living in a village as I do, one gets to know so much about human nature. But really you have made me quite curious. Do tell me your problem.'

'I'm afraid it's terribly hackneyed—just buried treasure,' said Edward.

'Indeed? But that sounds most exciting!'

'I know. Like *Treasure Island*. But our problem lacks the usual romantic touches. No point on a chart indicated by a skull and crossbones, no directions like "four paces to the left, west by north". It's horribly prosaic—just where we ought to dig.'

'Have you tried at all?'

'I should say we'd dug about two solid square acres! The whole place is ready to be turned into a market garden. We're just discussing whether to grow vegetable marrows or potatoes.'

Charmian said rather abruptly, 'May we really tell you all about it?'

'But, of course, my dear.'

'Then let's find a peaceful spot. Come on, Edward.' She

led the way out of the overcrowded and smoke-laden room, and they went up the stairs, to a small sitting-room on the second floor.

When they were seated, Charmian began abruptly. 'Well, here goes! The story starts with Uncle Mathew, uncle—or rather, great-great-uncle—to both of us. He was incredibly ancient. Edward and I were his only relations. He was fond of us and always declared that when he died he would leave his money between us. Well, he died last March and left everything he had to be divided equally between Edward and myself. What I've just said sounds rather callous—I don't mean that it was right that he died—actually we were very fond of him. But he'd been ill for some time.

'The point is that the "everything" he left turned out to be practically nothing at all. And that, frankly, was a bit of a blow to us both, wasn't it, Edward?'

The amiable Edward agreed. 'You see,' he said, 'we'd counted on it a bit. I mean, when you know a good bit of money is coming to you, you don't—well—buckle down and try to make it yourself. I'm in the army—not got anything to speak of outside my pay—and Charmian herself hasn't got a bean. She works as a stage manager in a repertory theatre—quite interesting, and she enjoys it—but no money in it. We'd counted on getting married, but weren't worried about the money side of it because we both knew we'd be jolly well off some day.'

'And now, you see, we're not!' said Charmian. 'What's more, Ansteys—that's the family place, and Edward and I both love it—will probably have to be sold. And Edward and I feel we just can't bear that! But if we don't find Uncle Mathew's money, we shall have to sell.'

Edward said, 'You know, Charmian, we still haven't come to the vital point.'

'Well, you talk, then.'

Edward turned to Miss Marple. 'It's like this, you see. As Uncle Mathew grew older, he got more and more suspicious. He didn't trust anybody.'

'Very wise of him,' said Miss Marple. 'The depravity of human nature is unbelievable.'

'Well, you may be right. Anyway, Uncle Mathew thought so. He had a friend who lost his money in a bank, and another friend who was ruined by an absconding solicitor, and he lost some money himself in a fraudulent company. He got so that he used to hold forth at great length that the only safe and sane thing to do was to convert your money into solid bullion and bury it.'

'Ah,' said Miss Marple. 'I begin to see.'

'Yes. Friends argued with him, pointed out that he'd get no interest that way, but he held that that didn't really matter. The bulk of your money, he said, should be "kept in a box under the bed or buried in the garden". Those were his words.'

Charmian went on. 'And when he died, he left hardly anything at all in securities, though he was very rich. So we think that that's what he must have done.'

Edward explained. 'We found that he had sold securities and drawn out large sums of money from time to time, and nobody knows what he did with them. But it seems probable that he lived up to his principles, and that he did buy gold and bury it.'

'He didn't say anything before he died? Leave any paper? No letter?'

'That's the maddening part of it. He didn't. He'd been unconscious for some days, but he rallied before he died. He looked at us both and chuckled—a faint, weak little chuckle. He said, "*You'll* be all right, my pretty pair of doves." And then he tapped his eye—his right eye—and winked at us. And then—he died. Poor old Uncle Mathew.'

'He tapped his eye,' said Miss Marple thoughtfully.

Edward said eagerly. 'Does that convey anything to you? It made me think of an Arsene Lupin story where there was something hidden in a man's glass eye. But Uncle Mathew didn't have a glass eye.'

Miss Marple shook her head. 'No—I can't think of anything at the moment.'

Charmian said disappointedly, 'Jane told us you'd say *at once* where to dig!'

Miss Marple smiled. 'I'm not quite a conjurer, you know. I didn't know your uncle, or what sort of man he was, and I don't know the house or the grounds.'

Charmian said, 'If you did know them?'

'Well, it must be quite simple, really, mustn't it?' said Miss Marple.

'Simple!' said Charmian. 'You come down to Ansteys and see if it's simple!'

It is possible that she did not mean the invitation to be taken seriously, but Miss Marple said briskly, 'Well, really, my dear, that's very kind of you. I've always wanted to have the chance of looking for buried treasure. And,' she added, looking at them with a beaming, late-Victorian smile, 'with a love interest, too!'

'You see!' said Charmian, gesturing dramatically.

They had just completed a grand tour of Ansteys. They had been round the kitchen garden—heavily trenched. They had been through the little woods, where every important tree had been dug round, and had gazed sadly on the pitted surface of the once smooth lawn. They had been up to the attic, where old trunks and chests had been rifled of their contents. They had been down to the cellars, where flagstones had been heaved unwillingly from their sockets. They had measured and tapped walls, and Miss Marple had been shown every antique piece of furniture that contained or could be suspected of containing a secret drawer.

On a table in the morning-room there was a heap of papers—all the papers that the late Mathew Stroud had left. Not one had been destroyed, and Charmian and Edward were wont to return to them again and again, earnestly perusing bills, invitations, and business correspondence in the hope of spotting a hitherto unnoticed clue.

'Can you think of anywhere we haven't looked?' demanded Charmian hopefully.

Miss Marple shook her head. 'You seem to have been very thorough, my dear. Perhaps, if I may say so, just a little *too* thorough. I always think, you know, that one should have a plan. It's like my friend, Mrs Eldritch, she had such a nice little maid, polished linoleum beautifully, but she was so thorough that she polished the bathroom floor too much, and as Mrs Eldritch was stepping out of the bath the cork mat slipped from under her, and she had a very nasty fall and actually broke her leg! Most awkward, because the bathroom door was locked, of course, and the gardener had to get a ladder and come in through the window—terribly distressing to Mrs Eldritch, who had always been a very modest woman.'

Edward moved restlessly.

Miss Marple said quickly, 'Please forgive me. So apt, I know, to fly off at a tangent. But one thing does remind one of another. And sometimes that is helpful. All I was trying to say was that perhaps if we tried to sharpen our wits and think of a likely place—'

Edward said crossly, 'You think of one, Miss Marple. Charmian's brains and mine are now only beautiful blanks!'

'Dear, dear. Of course—most tiring for you. If you don't mind I'll just look through all this.' She indicated the papers on the table. 'That is, if there's nothing private—I don't want to appear to pry.'

'Oh, that's all right. But I'm afraid you won't find anything.'

She sat down by the table and methodically worked through the sheaf of documents. As she replaced each one, she sorted them automatically into tidy little heaps. When she had finished she sat staring in front of her for some minutes.

Edward asked, not without a touch of malice, 'Well, Miss Marple?'

Miss Marple came to herself with a little start. 'I beg your pardon. Most helpful.'

'You've found something relevant?'

'Oh, no, nothing like that, but I do believe I know what sort of man your Uncle Mathew was. Rather like my own Uncle Henry, I think. Fond of rather obvious jokes. A bachelor, evidently—I wonder why—perhaps an early disappointment? Methodical up to a point, but not very fond of being tied up—so few bachelors are!'

Behind Miss Marple's back, Charmian made a sign to Edward. It said, *She's ga-ga*.

Miss Marple was continuing happily to talk of her deceased Uncle Henry. 'Very fond of puns, he was. And to some people, puns are most annoying. A mere play upon words may be very irritating. He was a suspicious man, too. Always was convinced the servants were robbing him. And sometimes, of course, they were, but not always. It grew upon him, poor man. Towards the end he suspected them of tampering with his food, and finally refused to eat anything but boiled eggs! Said nobody could tamper with the inside of a boiled egg. Dear Uncle Henry, he used to be such a merry soul at one time—very fond of his coffee after dinner. He always used to say, "This coffee is very Moorish," meaning, you know, that he'd like a little more.'

Edward felt that if he heard any more about Uncle Henry he'd go mad.

'Fond of young people, too,' went on Miss Marple, 'but inclined to tease them a little, if you know what I mean. Used to put bags of sweets where a child just couldn't reach them.'

Casting politeness aside, Charmian said, 'I think he sounds horrible!'

'Oh, no, dear, just an old bachelor, you know, and not used to children. And he wasn't at all stupid, really. He used to keep a good deal of money in the house, and he had a safe put in. Made a great fuss about it—and how very secure it was. As a result of his talking so much, burglars broke in one night and actually cut a hole in the safe with a chemical device.'

'Served him right,' said Edward.

'Oh, but there was nothing in the safe,' said Miss Marple. 'You see, he really kept the money somewhere else—behind some volumes of sermons in the library, as a matter of fact. He said people never took a book of that kind out of the shelf!'

Edward interrupted excitedly. 'I say, that's an idea. What about the library?'

But Charmian shook a scornful head. 'Do you think I hadn't thought of that? I went through all the books Tuesday of last week, when you went off to Portsmouth. Took them all out, shook them. Nothing there.'

Edward sighed. Then, rousing himself, he endeavoured to rid himself tactfully of their disappointing guest. 'It's been awfully good of you to come down as you have and try to help us. Sorry it's been all a wash-out. Feel we trespassed a lot on your time. However—I'll get the car out, and you'll be able to catch the three-thirty—'

'Oh,' said Miss Marple, 'but we've got to find the money, haven't we? You mustn't give up, Mr Rossiter. "If at first you don't succeed, try, try, try again."'

'You mean you're going to—go on trying?'

'Strictly speaking,' said Miss Marple, 'I haven't begun yet. "First catch your hare—" as Mrs Beaton says in her cookery book—a wonderful book but terribly expensive; most of the recipes begin, "Take a quart of cream and a dozen eggs." Let me see, where was I? Oh, yes. Well, we have, so to speak, caught our hare—the hare being, of course, your Uncle Mathew, and we've only got to decide now where he would have hidden the money. It ought to be quite simple.'

'Simple?' demanded Charmian.

'Oh, yes, dear. I'm sure he would have done the obvious thing. A secret drawer—that's my solution.'

Edward said dryly, 'You couldn't put bars of gold in a secret drawer.'

'No, no, of course not. But there's no reason to believe the money is in gold.'

'He always used to say—'

'So did my Uncle Henry about his safe! So I should strongly suspect that that was just a blind. Diamonds—now they could be in a secret drawer quite easily.'

'But we've looked in all the secret drawers. We had a cabinetmaker over to examine the furniture.'

'Did you, dear? That was clever of you. I should suggest your uncle's own desk would be the most likely. Was it the tall escritoire against the wall there?'

'Yes. And I'll show you.' Charmian went over to it. She took down the flap. Inside were pigeonholes and little drawers. She opened a small door in the centre and touched a spring inside the left-hand drawer. The bottom of the centre recess clicked and slid forward. Charmian drew it out, revealing a shallow well beneath. It was empty.

'Now isn't that a coincidence?' exclaimed Miss Marple. 'Uncle Henry had a desk just like this, only his was burr walnut and this is mahogany.'

'At any rate,' said Charmian, 'there's nothing there, as you can see.'

'I expect,' said Miss Marple, 'your cabinetmaker was a young man. He didn't know everything. People were very artful when they made hiding-places in those days. There's such a thing as a secret inside a secret.'

She extracted a hairpin from her neat bun of grey hair. Straightening it out, she stuck the point into what appeared to be a tiny wormhole in one side of the secret recess. With a little difficulty she pulled out a small drawer. In it was a bundle of faded letters and a folded paper.

Edward and Charmian pounced on the find together. With trembling fingers Edward unfolded the paper. He dropped it with an exclamation of disgust.

'A damned cookery recipe. Baked ham!'

Charmian was untying a ribbon that held the letters together. She drew one out and glanced at it. 'Love letters!'

Miss Marple reacted with Victorian gusto. 'How interesting! Perhaps the reason your uncle never married.'

Charmian read aloud:

'"My ever dear Mathew, I must confess that the time seems long indeed since I received your last letter. I try to occupy myself with the various tasks allotted to me, and often say to myself that I am indeed fortunate to see

so much of the globe, though little did I think when I went to America that I should voyage off to these far islands!"'

Charmian broke off. 'Where is it from? Oh! Hawaii!' She went on:

'"Alas, these natives are still far from seeing the light. They are in an unclothed and savage state and spend most of their time swimming and dancing, adorning themselves with garlands of flowers. Mr Gray has made some converts but it is uphill work, and he and Mrs Gray get sadly discouraged. I try to do all I can to cheer and encourage him, but I, too, am often sad for a reason you can guess, dear Mathew. Alas, absence is a severe trial for a loving heart. Your renewed vows and protestations of affection cheered me greatly. Now and always you have my faithful and devoted heart, dear Mathew, and I remain—Your true love, Betty Martin.

'"PS—I address my letter under cover to our mutual friend, Matilda Graves, as usual. I hope heaven will pardon this little subterfuge."'

Edward whistled. 'A female missionary! So that was Uncle Mathew's romance. I wonder why they never married?'

'She seems to have gone all over the world,' said Charmian, looking through the letters. 'Mauritius—all sorts of places. Probably died of yellow fever or something.'

A gentle chuckle made them start. Miss Marple was

apparently much amused. 'Well, well,' she said. 'Fancy that, now!'

She was reading the recipe for baked ham. Seeing their enquiring glances, she read out: '"Baked ham with spinach. Take a nice piece of gammon, stuff with cloves, and cover with brown sugar. Bake in a slow oven. Serve with a border of pureed spinach." What do you think of that, now?'

'I think it sounds filthy,' said Edward.

'No, no, actually it would be very good—but what do you think of *the whole thing*?'

A sudden ray of light illuminated Edward's face. 'Do you think it's a code—cryptogram of some kind?' He seized it. 'Look here, Charmian, it might be, you know! No reason to put a cooking-recipe in a secret drawer otherwise.'

'Exactly,' said Miss Marple. 'Very, very significant.'

Charmian said, 'I know what it might be—invisible ink! Let's heat it. Turn on the electric fire.'

Edward did so, but no signs of writing appeared under the treatment.

Miss Marple coughed. 'I really think, you know, that you're making it rather *too* difficult. The recipe is only an indication, so to speak. It is, I think, the letters that are significant.'

'The letters?'

'Especially,' said Miss Marple, 'the signature.'

But Edward hardly heard her. He called excitedly, 'Charmian! Come here! She's right. See—the envelopes are old, right enough, but the letters themselves were written much later.'

'Exactly,' said Miss Marple.

'They're only fake old. I bet anything old Uncle Mat faked them himself—'

'Precisely,' said Miss Marple.

'The whole thing's a sell. There never was a female missionary. It must be a code.'

'My dear, dear children—there's really no need to make it all so difficult. Your uncle was really a very simple man. He had to have his little joke, that was all.'

For the first time they gave her their full attention.

'Just exactly what do you mean, Miss Marple?' asked Charmian.

'I mean, dear, that you're actually holding the money in your hand this minute.'

Charmian stared down.

'The signature, dear. That gives the whole thing away. The recipe is just an indication. Shorn of all the cloves and brown sugar and the rest of it, what is it *actually*? Why, gammon and spinach to be sure! *Gammon and spinach!* Meaning—nonsense! So it's clear that it's the letters that are important. And then, if you take into consideration what your uncle did just before he died. He tapped his eye, you said. Well, there you are—that gives you the clue, you see.'

Charmian said, 'Are we mad, or are you?'

'Surely, my dear, you must have heard the expression meaning that something is not a true picture, or has it quite died out nowadays? "All my eye and Betty Martin."'

Edward gasped, his eyes falling to the letter in his hand. 'Betty Martin—'

'Of course, Mr Rossiter. As you have just said, there

isn't—there wasn't any such person. The letters were written by your uncle, and I dare say he got a lot of fun out of writing them! As you say, the writing on the envelopes is much older—in fact, the envelope couldn't belong to the letters, anyway, because the postmark of one you are holding is eighteen fifty-one.'

She paused. She made it very emphatic. 'Eighteen fifty-one. And that explains everything, doesn't it?'

'Not to me,' said Edward.

'Well, of course,' said Miss Marple, 'I dare say it wouldn't to me if it weren't for my great-nephew Lionel. Such a dear little boy and a passionate stamp collector. Knows all about stamps. It was he who told me about the rare and expensive stamps and that a wonderful new find had come up for auction. And I actually remember his mentioning one stamp—an eighteen fifty-one *blue two-cent*. It realized something like twenty-five thousand dollars, I believe. Fancy! I should imagine that the other stamps are something also rare and expensive. No doubt your uncle bought through dealers and was careful to "cover his tracks", as they say in detective stories.'

Edward groaned. He sat down and buried his face in his hands.

'What's the matter?' demanded Charmian.

'Nothing. It's only the awful thought that, but for Miss Marple, we might have burned these letters in a decent, gentlemanly way!'

'Ah,' said Miss Marple, 'that's just what these old gentlemen who are fond of their jokes never realize. Uncle Henry, I remember, sent a favourite niece a five-pound note for a Christmas present. He put it in a Christmas card, gummed the card together, and wrote on it, "Love and best wishes. Afraid this is all I can manage this year."'

'She, poor girl, was annoyed at what she thought was his meanness and threw it all straight into the fire; then, of course, he had to give her another.'

Edward's feelings towards Uncle Henry had suffered an abrupt and complete change.

'Miss Marple,' he said, 'I'm going to get a bottle of champagne. We'll all drink the health of your Uncle Henry.'

Tape-Measure Murder

Miss Politt took hold of the knocker and rapped politely on the cottage door. After a discreet interval she knocked again. The parcel under her left arm shifted a little as she did so, and she readjusted it. Inside the parcel was Mrs Spenlow's new green winter dress, ready for fitting. From Miss Politt's left hand dangled a bag of black silk, containing a tape measure, a pincushion, and a large, practical pair of scissors.

Miss Politt was tall and gaunt, with a sharp nose, pursed lips, and meagre iron-grey hair. She hesitated before using the knocker for the third time. Glancing down the street, she saw a figure rapidly approaching. Miss Hartnell, jolly, weather-beaten, fifty-five, shouted out in her usual loud bass voice, 'Good afternoon, Miss Politt!'

The dressmaker answered, 'Good afternoon, Miss Hartnell.' Her voice was excessively thin and genteel in its accents. She had started life as a lady's maid. 'Excuse me,' she went on, 'but do you happen to know if by any chance Mrs Spenlow isn't at home?'

'Not the least idea,' said Miss Hartnell.

'It's rather awkward, you see. I was to fit on Mrs Spenlow's new dress this afternoon. Three-thirty, she said.'

Miss Hartnell consulted her wrist watch. 'It's a little past the half-hour now.'

'Yes. I have knocked three times, but there doesn't seem to be any answer, so I was wondering if perhaps Mrs Spenlow might have gone out and forgotten. She doesn't forget appointments as a rule, and she wants the dress to wear the day after tomorrow.'

Miss Hartnell entered the gate and walked up the path to join Miss Politt outside the door of Laburnum Cottage.

'Why doesn't Gladys answer the door?' she demanded. 'Oh, no, of course, it's Thursday—Gladys's day out. I expect Mrs Spenlow has fallen asleep. I don't expect you've made enough noise with this thing.'

Seizing the knocker, she executed a deafening *rat-a-tat-tat*, and in addition thumped upon the panels of the door. She also called out in a stentorian voice, 'What ho, within there!'

There was no response.

Miss Politt murmured, 'Oh, I think Mrs Spenlow must have forgotten and gone out. I'll call round some other time.' She began edging away down the path.

'Nonsense,' said Miss Hartnell firmly. 'She can't have gone out. I'd have met her. I'll just take a look through the windows and see if I can find any signs of life.'

She laughed in her usual hearty manner, to indicate that it was a joke, and applied a perfunctory glance to the nearest window-pane—perfunctory because she knew quite well that the front room was seldom used, Mr and Mrs Spenlow preferring the small back sitting-room.

Perfunctory as it was, though, it succeeded in its object. Miss Hartnell, it is true, saw no signs of life. On the contrary, she saw, through the window, Mrs Spenlow lying on the hearthrug—dead.

'Of course,' said Miss Hartnell, telling the story afterwards, 'I managed to keep my head. That Politt creature wouldn't have had the least idea of what to do. "Got to keep our heads," I said to her. "*You* stay here, and I'll go for Constable Palk." She said something about not wanting to be left, but I paid no attention at all. One has to be firm with that sort of person. I've always found they enjoy making a fuss. So I was just going off when, at that very moment, Mr Spenlow came round the corner of the house.'

Here Miss Hartnell made a significant pause. It enabled her audience to ask breathlessly, 'Tell me, how did he *look*?'

Miss Hartnell would then go on, 'Frankly, *I* suspected something at once! He was *far* too calm. He didn't seem surprised in the least. And you may say what you like, it isn't natural for a man to hear that his wife is dead and display no emotion whatever.'

Everybody agreed with this statement.

The police agreed with it, too. So suspicious did they consider Mr Spenlow's detachment, that they lost no time in ascertaining how that gentleman was situated as a result of his wife's death. When they discovered that Mrs Spenlow had been the monied partner, and that her money went to her husband under a will made soon after their marriage, they were more suspicious than ever.

Miss Marple, that sweet-faced—and, some said, vinegar-tongued—elderly spinster who lived in the house next to the rectory, was interviewed very early—within half an hour of the discovery of the crime. She was approached by Police Constable Palk, importantly thumbing a note-book. 'If you don't mind, ma'am, I've a few questions to ask you.'

Miss Marple said, 'In connection with the murder of Mrs Spenlow?'

Palk was startled. 'May I ask, madam, how you got to know of it?'

'The fish,' said Miss Marple.

The reply was perfectly intelligible to Constable Palk. He assumed correctly that the fishmonger's boy had brought it, together with Miss Marple's evening meal.

Miss Marple continued gently. 'Lying on the floor in the sitting-room, strangled—possibly by a very narrow belt. But whatever it was, it was taken away.'

Palk's face was wrathful. 'How that young Fred gets to know everything—'

Miss Marple cut him short adroitly. She said, 'There's a pin in your tunic.'

Constable Palk looked down, startled. He said, 'They do say, "See a pin and pick it up, all the day you'll have good luck."'

'I hope that will come true. Now what is it you want me to tell you?'

Constable Palk cleared his throat, looked important, and consulted his notebook. 'Statement was made to me by Mr Arthur Spenlow, husband of the deceased. Mr Spenlow says that at two-thirty, as far as he can say, he was rung up by Miss Marple, and asked if he would come over at a quarter past three as she was anxious to consult him about something. Now, ma'am, is that true?'

'Certainly not,' said Miss Marple.

'You did not ring up Mr Spenlow at two-thirty?'

'Neither at two-thirty nor any other time.'

'Ah,' said Constable Palk, and sucked his moustache with a good deal of satisfaction.

'What else did Mr Spenlow say?'

'Mr Spenlow's statement was that he came over here as requested, leaving his own house at ten minutes past three; that on arrival here he was informed by the maid-servant that Miss Marple was "not at 'ome".'

'That part of it is true,' said Miss Marple. 'He did come here, but I was at a meeting at the Women's Institute.'

'Ah,' said Constable Palk again.

Miss Marple exclaimed, 'Do tell me, Constable, do you suspect Mr Spenlow?'

'It's not for me to say at this stage, but it looks to me as though somebody, naming no names, has been trying to be artful.'

Miss Marple said thoughtfully, 'Mr Spenlow?'

She liked Mr Spenlow. He was a small, spare man, stiff and conventional in speech, the acme of respectability. It seemed odd that he should have come to live in the country, he had so clearly lived in towns all his life. To Miss Marple he confided the reason. He said, 'I have always intended, ever since I was a small boy, to live in the country some day and have a garden of my own. I have always been very much attached to flowers. My wife, you know, kept a flower shop. That's where I saw her first.'

A dry statement, but it opened up a vista of romance. A younger, prettier Mrs Spenlow, seen against a background of flowers.

Mr Spenlow, however, really knew nothing about flowers. He had no idea of seeds, of cuttings, of bedding out, of annuals or perennials. He had only a vision—a vision of a small cottage garden thickly planted with sweet-smelling, brightly coloured blossoms. He had asked, almost pathetically, for instruction, and had noted down Miss Marple's replies to questions in a little book.

He was a man of quiet method. It was, perhaps, because of this trait, that the police were interested in him when his wife was found murdered. With patience and perseverance they learned a good deal about the late Mrs Spenlow—and soon all St Mary Mead knew it, too.

The late Mrs Spenlow had begun life as a between-maid in a large house. She had left that position to marry the second gardener, and with him had started a flower shop in London. The shop had prospered. Not so the gardener, who before long had sickened and died.

His widow carried on the shop and enlarged it in an ambitious way. She had continued to prosper. Then she had sold the business at a handsome price and embarked upon matrimony for the second time—with Mr Spenlow, a middle-aged jeweller who had inherited a small and struggling business. Not long afterwards, they had sold the business and came down to St Mary Mead.

Mrs Spenlow was a well-to-do woman. The profits from

her florist's establishment she had invested—'under spirit guidance', as she explained to all and sundry. The spirits had advised her with unexpected acumen.

All her investments had prospered, some in quite a sensational fashion. Instead, however, of this increasing her belief in spiritualism, Mrs Spenlow basely deserted mediums and sittings, and made a brief but wholehearted plunge into an obscure religion with Indian affinities which was based on various forms of deep breathing. When, however, she arrived at St Mary Mead, she had relapsed into a period of orthodox Church-of-England beliefs. She was a good deal at the vicarage, and attended church services with assiduity. She patronized the village shops, took an interest in the local happenings, and played village bridge.

A humdrum, everyday life. And—suddenly—murder.

Colonel Melchett, the chief constable, had summoned Inspector Slack.

Slack was a positive type of man. When he had made up his mind, he was sure. He was quite sure now. 'Husband did it, sir,' he said.

'You think so?'

'Quite sure of it. You've only got to look at him. Guilty as hell. Never showed a sign of grief or emotion. He came back to the house knowing she was dead.'

'Wouldn't he at least have tried to act the part of the distracted husband?'

'Not him, sir. Too pleased with himself. Some gentlemen can't act. Too stiff.'

'Any other woman in his life?' Colonel Melchett asked.

'Haven't been able to find any trace of one. Of course, he's the artful kind. He'd cover his tracks. As I see it, he was just fed up with his wife. She'd got the money, and I should say was a trying woman to live with—always taking up with some "ism" or other. He cold-bloodedly decided to do away with her and live comfortably on his own.'

'Yes, that could be the case, I suppose.'

'Depend upon it, that was it. Made his plans careful. Pretended to get a phone call—'

Melchett interrupted him. 'No call been traced?'

'No, sir. That means either that he lied, or that the call was put through from a public telephone booth. The only two public phones in the village are at the station and the post office. Post office it certainly wasn't. Mrs Blade sees everyone who comes in. Station it might be. Train arrives at two twenty-seven and there's a bit of a bustle then. But the main thing is *he* says it was Miss Marple who called him up, and that certainly isn't true. The call didn't come from her house, and she herself was away at the Institute.'

'You're not overlooking the possibility that the husband was deliberately got out of the way—by someone who wanted to murder Mrs Spenlow?'

'You're thinking of young Ted Gerard, aren't you, sir? I've been working on him—what we're up against there is lack of motive. He doesn't stand to gain anything.'

'He's an undesirable character, though. Quite a pretty little spot of embezzlement to his credit.'

'I'm not saying he isn't a wrong 'un. Still, he did go to

his boss and own up to that embezzlement. And his employers weren't wise to it.'

'An Oxford Grouper,' said Melchett.

'Yes, sir. Became a convert and went off to do the straight thing and own up to having pinched money. I'm not saying, mind you, that it mayn't have been astuteness. He may have thought he was suspected and decided to gamble on honest repentance.'

'You have a sceptical mind, Slack,' said Colonel Melchett. 'By the way, have you talked to Miss Marple at all?'

'What's *she* got to do with it, sir?'

'Oh, nothing. But she hears things, you know. Why don't you go and have a chat with her? She's a very sharp old lady.'

Slack changed the subject. 'One thing I've been meaning to ask you, sir. That domestic-service job where the deceased started her career—Sir Robert Abercrombie's place. That's where that jewel robbery was—emeralds—worth a packet. Never got them. I've been looking it up—must have happened when the Spenlow woman was there, though she'd have been quite a girl at the time. Don't think she was mixed up in it, do you, sir? Spenlow, you know, was one of those little tuppenny-ha'penny jewellers—just the chap for a fence.'

Melchett shook his head. 'Don't think there's anything in that. She didn't even know Spenlow at the time. I remember the case. Opinion in police circles was that a son of the house was mixed up in it—Jim Abercrombie—awful young waster. Had a pile of debts, and just after the robbery they were all paid off—some rich woman, so they said, but I don't know—Old Abercrombie hedged a bit about the case—tried to call the police off.'

'It was just an idea, sir,' said Slack.

Miss Marple received Inspector Slack with gratification, especially when she heard that he had been sent by Colonel Melchett.

'Now, really, that is very kind of Colonel Melchett. I didn't know he remembered me.'

'He remembers you, all right. Told me that what you didn't know of what goes on in St Mary Mead isn't worth knowing.'

'Too kind of him, but really I don't know anything at all. About this murder, I mean.'

'You know what the talk about it is.'

'Oh, of course—but it wouldn't do, would it, to repeat just idle talk?'

Slack said, with an attempt at geniality, 'This isn't an official conversation, you know. It's in confidence, so to speak.'

'You mean you really want to know what people are saying? Whether there's any truth in it or not?'

'That's the idea.'

'Well, of course, there's been a great deal of talk and speculation. And there are really two distinct camps, if you understand me. To begin with, there are the people who think that the husband did it. A husband or a wife is, in a way, the natural person to suspect, don't you think so?'

'Maybe,' said the inspector cautiously.

'Such close quarters, you know. Then, so often, the money angle. I hear that it was Mrs Spenlow who had the money, and therefore Mr Spenlow does benefit by her death. In this wicked world I'm afraid the most uncharitable assumptions are often justified.'

'He comes into a tidy sum, all right.'

'Just so. It would seem quite plausible, wouldn't it, for him to strangle her, leave the house by the back, come across the fields to my house, ask for me and pretend he'd had a telephone call from me, then go back and find his wife murdered in his absence—hoping, of course, that the crime would be put down to some tramp or burglar.'

The inspector nodded. 'What with the money angle—and if they'd been on bad terms lately—'

But Miss Marple interrupted him. 'Oh, but they hadn't.'

'You know that for a fact?'

'Everyone would have known if they'd quarrelled! The maid, Gladys Brent—she'd have soon spread it round the village.'

The inspector said feebly, 'She mightn't have known—' and received a pitying smile in reply.

Miss Marple went on. 'And then there's the other school of thought. Ted Gerard. A good-looking young man. I'm afraid, you know, that good looks are inclined to influence one more than they should. Our last curate but one—quite a magical effect! All the girls came to church—evening service as well as morning. And many older women became unusually active in parish work—and the slippers and scarfs that were made for him! Quite embarrassing for the poor young man.

'But let me see, where was I? Oh, yes, this young man, Ted Gerard. Of course, there has been talk about him. He's come down to see her so often. Though Mrs Spenlow told me herself that he was a member of what I think they call the Oxford Group. A religious movement. They are quite sincere and very earnest, I believe, and Mrs Spenlow was impressed by it all.'

Miss Marple took a breath and went on. 'And I'm sure there was no reason to believe that there was anything more in it than that, but you know what people are. Quite a lot of people are convinced that Mrs Spenlow was infatuated with the young man, and that she'd lent him quite a lot of money. And it's perfectly true that he was actually seen at the station that day. In the train—the two twenty-seven down train. But of course it would be quite easy, wouldn't it, to slip out of the other side of the train and go through the cutting and over the fence and round by the hedge and never come out of the station entrance at all. So that he need not have been seen going to the cottage. And, of course, people do think that what Mrs Spenlow was wearing was rather peculiar.'

'Peculiar?'

'A kimono. Not a dress.' Miss Marple blushed. 'That sort of thing, you know, is, perhaps, rather suggestive to some people.'

'You think it was suggestive?'

'Oh, no, *I* don't think so, I think it was perfectly natural.'

'You think it was natural?'

'Under the circumstances, yes.' Miss Marple's glance was cool and reflective.

Inspector Slack said, 'It might give us another motive for the husband. Jealousy.'

'Oh, no, Mr Spenlow would never be jealous. He's not the sort of man who notices things. If his wife had gone away and left a note on the pincushion, it would be the first he'd know of anything of that kind.'

Inspector Slack was puzzled by the intent way she was looking at him. He had an idea that all her conversation was intended to hint at something he didn't understand. She said now, with some emphasis, 'Didn't *you* find any clues, Inspector—on the spot?'

'People don't leave fingerprints and cigarette ash nowadays, Miss Marple.'

'But this, I think,' she suggested, 'was an old-fashioned crime—'

Slack said sharply, 'Now what do you mean by that?'

Miss Marple remarked slowly, 'I think, you know, that Constable Palk could help you. He was the first person on the—on the "scene of the crime", as they say.'

Mr Spenlow was sitting in a deck chair. He looked bewildered. He said, in his thin, precise voice, 'I may, of course, be imagining what occurred. My hearing is not as good as it was. But I distinctly think I heard a small boy call after me, "Yah, who's a Crippen?" It—it conveyed the impression to me that he was of the opinion that I had—had killed my dear wife.'

Miss Marple, gently snipping off a dead rose head, said, 'That was the impression he meant to convey, no doubt.'

'But what could possibly have put such an idea into a child's head?'

Miss Marple coughed. 'Listening, no doubt, to the opinions of his elders.'

'You—you really mean that other people think that, also?'

'Quite half the people in St Mary Mead.'

'But—my dear lady—what can possibly have given rise to such an idea? I was sincerely attached to my wife. She did not, alas, take to living in the country as much as I had hoped she would do, but perfect agreement on every subject is an impossible idea. I assure you I feel her loss very keenly.'

'Probably. But if you will excuse my saying so, you don't sound as though you do.'

Mr Spenlow drew his meagre frame up to its full height. 'My dear lady, many years ago I read of a certain Chinese philosopher who, when his dearly loved wife was taken from him, continued calmly to beat a gong in the street—a customary Chinese pastime, I presume—exactly as usual. The people of the city were much impressed by his fortitude.'

'But,' said Miss Marple, 'the people of St Mary Mead react rather differently. Chinese philosophy does not appeal to them.'

'But you understand?'

Miss Marple nodded. 'My Uncle Henry,' she explained, 'was a man of unusual self-control. His motto was "Never display emotion". He, too, was very fond of flowers.'

'I was thinking,' said Mr Spenlow with something like eagerness, 'that I might, perhaps, have a pergola on the west side of the cottage. Pink roses and, perhaps, wisteria. And there is a white starry flower, whose name for the moment escapes me—'

In the tone in which she spoke to her grandnephew, aged three, Miss Marple said, 'I have a very nice catalogue here, with pictures. Perhaps you would like to look through it—I have to go up to the village.'

Leaving Mr Spenlow sitting happily in the garden with his catalogue, Miss Marple went up to her room, hastily rolled up a dress in a piece of brown paper, and, leaving the house, walked briskly up to the post office. Miss Politt, the dressmaker, lived in the rooms over the post office.

But Miss Marple did not at once go through the door and up the stairs. It was just two-thirty, and, a minute late, the Much Benham bus drew up outside the post office door. It was one of the events of the day in St Mary Mead. The postmistress hurried out with parcels, parcels connected with the shop side of her business, for the post office also dealt in sweets, cheap books, and children's toys.

For some four minutes Miss Marple was alone in the post office.

Not till the postmistress returned to her post did Miss Marple go upstairs and explain to Miss Politt that she wanted her old grey crepe altered and made more fashionable if that were possible. Miss Politt promised to see what she could do.

The chief constable was rather astonished when Miss Marple's name was brought to him. She came in with many apologies. 'So sorry—so very sorry to disturb you. You are so busy, I know, but then you have always been so very kind, Colonel Melchett, and I felt I would rather come to you instead of Inspector Slack. For one thing, you know, I should hate Constable Palk to get into any trouble. Strictly speaking, I suppose he shouldn't have touched anything at all.'

Colonel Melchett was slightly bewildered. He said, 'Palk? That's the St Mary Mead constable, isn't it? What has he been doing?'

'He picked up a pin, you know. It was in his tunic. And it occurred to me at the time that it was quite probable he had actually picked it up in Mrs Spenlow's house.'

'Quite, quite. But after all, you know, what's a pin? Matter of fact he did pick the pin up just by Mrs Spenlow's body. Came and told Slack about it yesterday—you put him up to that, I gather? Oughtn't to have touched anything, of course, but as I said, what's a pin? It was only a common pin. Sort of thing any woman might use.'

'Oh, no, Colonel Melchett, that's where you're wrong. To a man's eye, perhaps, it looked like an ordinary pin, but it wasn't. It was a special pin, a very thin pin, the kind you buy by the box, the kind used mostly by dressmakers.'

Melchett stared at her, a faint light of comprehension breaking in on him. Miss Marple nodded her head several times, eagerly.

'Yes, of course. It seems to me so obvious. She was in her kimono because she was going to try on her new dress, and she went into the front room, and Miss Politt just said something about measurements and put the tape measure round her neck—and then all she'd have to do was to cross it and pull—quite easy, so I've heard. And then, of course, she'd go outside and pull the door to and stand there knocking as though she'd just arrived. But the pin shows she'd *already been in the house*.'

'And it was Miss Politt who telephoned to Spenlow?'

'Yes. From the post office at two-thirty—just when the bus comes and the post office would be empty.'

Colonel Melchett said, 'But my dear Miss Marple, why? In heaven's name, why? You can't have a murder without a motive.'

'Well, I think, you know, Colonel Melchett, from all I've heard, that the crime dates from a long time back. It reminds me, you know, of my two cousins, Antony and Gordon. Whatever Antony did always went right for him, and with poor Gordon it was just the other way about. Race horses went lame, and stocks went down, and property depreciated. As I see it, the two women were in it together.'

'In what?'

'The robbery. Long ago. Very valuable emeralds, so I've heard. The lady's maid and the tweeny. Because one thing hasn't been explained—how, when the tweeny married the gardener, did they have enough money to set up a flower shop?

'The answer is, it was her share of the—the swag, I think is the right expression. Everything she did turned out well. Money made money. But the other one, the lady's maid, must have been unlucky. She came down to being just a village dressmaker. Then they met again. Quite all right at first, I expect, until Mr Ted Gerard came on the scene.

'Mrs Spenlow, you see, was already suffering from conscience, and was inclined to be emotionally religious. This young man no doubt urged her to "face up" and to "come clean" and I dare say she was strung up to do it. But Miss Politt didn't see it that way. All she saw was that she might go to prison for a robbery she had committed years ago. So she made up her mind to put a stop to it all. I'm afraid, you know, that she was always rather a wicked woman. I don't believe she'd have turned a hair if that nice, stupid Mr Spenlow had been hanged.'

Colonel Melchett said slowly, 'We can—er—verify your theory—up to a point. The identity of the Politt woman with the lady's maid at the Abercrombies', but—'

Miss Marple reassured him. 'It will be all quite easy. She's the kind of woman who will break down at once when she's taxed with the truth. And then, you see, I've got her tape measure. I—er—abstracted it yesterday when I was trying on. When she misses it and thinks the police have got it—well, she's quite an ignorant woman and she'll think it will prove the case against her in some way.'

She smiled at him encouragingly. 'You'll have no trouble, I can assure you.' It was the tone in which his favourite aunt had once assured him that he could not fail to pass his entrance examination into Sandhurst.

And he had passed.

The Case of the Caretaker

'Well,' demanded Doctor Haydock of his patient. 'And how goes it today?'

Miss Marple smiled at him wanly from pillows.

'I suppose, really, that I'm better,' she admitted, 'but I feel so terribly depressed. I can't help feeling how much better it would have been if I had died. After all, I'm an old woman. Nobody wants me or cares about me.'

Doctor Haydock interrupted with his usual brusqueness. 'Yes, yes, typical after-reaction of this type of flu. What you need is something to take you out of yourself. A mental tonic.'

Miss Marple sighed and shook her head.

'And what's more,' continued Doctor Haydock, 'I've brought my medicine with me!'

He tossed a long envelope on to the bed.

'Just the thing for you. The kind of puzzle that is right up your street.'

'A puzzle?' Miss Marple looked interested.

'Literary effort of mine,' said the doctor, blushing a little. 'Tried to make a regular story of it. "He said," "she said," "the girl thought," etc. Facts of the story are true.'

'But why a puzzle?' asked Miss Marple.

Doctor Haydock grinned. 'Because the interpretation is up to you. I want to see if you're as clever as you always make out.'

With that Parthian shot he departed.

Miss Marple picked up the manuscript and began to read.

'And where is the bride?' asked Miss Harmon genially.

The village was all agog to see the rich and beautiful young wife that Harry Laxton had brought back from abroad. There was a general indulgent feeling that Harry—wicked young scapegrace—had had all the luck. Everyone had always felt indulgent towards Harry. Even the owners of windows that had suffered from his indiscriminate use of a catapult had found their indignation dissipated by young Harry's abject expression of regret. He had broken windows, robbed orchards, poached rabbits, and later had run into debt, got entangled with the local tobacconist's daughter—been disentangled and sent off to Africa—and the village as represented by various ageing spinsters had murmured indulgently. 'Ah, well! Wild oats! He'll settle down!'

And now, sure enough, the prodigal had returned—not in affliction, but in triumph. Harry Laxton had 'made good' as the saying goes. He had pulled himself together, worked hard, and had finally met and successfully wooed a young Anglo-French girl who was the possessor of a considerable fortune.

Harry might have lived in London, or purchased an

estate in some fashionable hunting county, but he preferred to come back to the part of the world that was home to him. And there, in the most romantic way, he purchased the derelict estate in the dower house of which he had passed his childhood.

Kingsdean House had been unoccupied for nearly seventy years. It had gradually fallen into decay and abandon. An elderly caretaker and his wife lived in the one habitable corner of it. It was a vast, unprepossessing grandiose mansion, the gardens overgrown with rank vegetation and the trees hemming it in like some gloomy enchanter's den.

The dower house was a pleasant, unpretentious house and had been let for a long term of years to Major Laxton, Harry's father. As a boy, Harry had roamed over the Kingsdean estate and knew every inch of the tangled woods, and the old house itself had always fascinated him.

Major Laxton had died some years ago, so it might have been thought that Harry would have had no ties to bring him back—nevertheless it was to the home of his boyhood that Harry brought his bride. The ruined old Kingsdean House was pulled down. An army of builders and contractors swooped down upon the place, and in almost a miraculously short space of time—so marvellously does wealth tell—the new house rose white and gleaming among the trees.

Next came a posse of gardeners and after them a procession of furniture vans.

The house was ready. Servants arrived. Lastly, a costly

limousine deposited Harry and Mrs Harry at the front door.

The village rushed to call, and Mrs Price, who owned the largest house, and who considered herself to lead society in the place, sent out cards of invitation for a party 'to meet the bride'.

It was a great event. Several ladies had new frocks for the occasion. Everyone was excited, curious, anxious to see this fabulous creature. They said it was all so like a fairy story!

Miss Harmon, weather-beaten, hearty spinster, threw out her question as she squeezed her way through the crowded drawing-room door. Little Miss Brent, a thin, acidulated spinster, fluttered out information.

'Oh, my dear, quite charming. Such pretty manners. And quite young. Really, you know, it makes one feel quite envious to see someone who has everything like that. Good looks and money and breeding—most distinguished, nothing in the least common about her—and dear Harry so devoted!'

'Ah,' said Miss Harmon, 'it's early days yet!'

Miss Brent's thin nose quivered appreciatively. 'Oh, my dear, do you really think—'

'We all know what Harry is,' said Miss Harmon.

'We know what he was! But I expect now—'

'Ah,' said Miss Harmon, 'men are always the same. Once a gay deceiver, always a gay deceiver. I know them.'

'Dear, dear. Poor young thing.' Miss Brent looked much happier. 'Yes, I expect she'll have trouble with him.

Someone ought really to warn her. I wonder if she's heard anything of the old story?'

'It seems so very unfair,' said Miss Brent, 'that she should know nothing. So awkward. Especially with only the one chemist's shop in the village.'

For the erstwhile tobacconist's daughter was now married to Mr Edge, the chemist.

'It would be so much nicer,' said Miss Brent, 'if Mrs Laxton were to deal with Boots in Much Benham.'

'I dare say,' said Miss Harmon, 'that Harry Laxton will suggest that himself.'

And again a significant look passed between them.

'But I certainly think,' said Miss Harmon, 'that she ought to know.'

'Beasts!' said Clarice Vane indignantly to her uncle, Doctor Haydock. 'Absolute beasts some people are.'

He looked at her curiously.

She was a tall, dark girl, handsome, warm-hearted and impulsive. Her big brown eyes were alight now with indignation as she said, 'All these cats—saying things—hinting things.'

'About Harry Laxton?'

'Yes, about his affair with the tobacconist's daughter.'

'Oh, that!' The doctor shrugged his shoulders. 'A great many young men have affairs of that kind.'

'Of course they do. And it's all over. So why harp on it? And bring it up years after? It's like ghouls feasting on dead bodies.'

'I dare say, my dear, it does seem like that to you. But you see, they have very little to talk about down here, and so I'm afraid they do tend to dwell upon past scandals. But I'm curious to know why it upsets you so much?'

Clarice Vane bit her lip and flushed. She said, in a curiously muffled voice. 'They—they look so happy. The Laxtons, I mean. They're young and in love, and it's all so lovely for them. I hate to think of it being spoiled by whispers and hints and innuendoes and general beastliness.'

'H'm. I see.'

Clarice went on. 'He was talking to me just now. He's so happy and eager and excited and—yes, thrilled—at having got his heart's desire and rebuilt Kingsdean. He's like a child about it all. And she—well, I don't suppose anything has ever gone wrong in her whole life. She's always had everything. You've seen her. What did you think of her?'

The doctor did not answer at once. For other people, Louise Laxton might be an object of envy. A spoiled darling of fortune. To him she had brought only the refrain of a popular song heard many years ago, Poor little rich girl—

A small, delicate figure, with flaxen hair curled rather stiffly round her face and big, wistful blue eyes.

Louise was drooping a little. The long stream of congratulations had tired her. She was hoping it might soon be time to go. Perhaps, even now, Harry might say so. She looked at him sideways. So tall and broad-shouldered with his eager pleasure in this horrible, dull party.

Poor little rich girl—

'Ooph!' It was a sigh of relief.

Harry turned to look at his wife amusedly. They were driving away from the party.

She said, 'Darling, what a frightful party!'

Harry laughed. 'Yes, pretty terrible. Never mind, my sweet. It had to be done, you know. All these old pussies knew me when I lived here as a boy. They'd have been terribly disappointed not to have got a look at you close up.'

Louise made a grimace. She said, 'Shall we have to see a lot of them?'

'What? Oh, no. They'll come and make ceremonious calls with card cases, and you'll return the calls and then you needn't bother any more. You can have your own friends down or whatever you like.'

Louise said, after a minute or two, 'Isn't there anyone amusing living down here?'

'Oh, yes. There's the County, you know. Though you may find them a bit dull, too. Mostly interested in bulbs and dogs and horses. You'll ride, of course. You'll enjoy that. There's a horse over at Eglinton I'd like you to see. A beautiful animal, perfectly trained, no vice in him but plenty of spirit.'

The car slowed down to take the turn into the gates

of Kingsdean. Harry wrenched the wheel and swore as a grotesque figure sprang up in the middle of the road and he only just managed to avoid it. It stood there, shaking a fist and shouting after them.

Louise clutched his arm. 'Who's that—that horrible old woman?'

Harry's brow was black. 'That's old Murgatroyd. She and her husband were caretakers in the old house. They were there for nearly thirty years.'

'Why does she shake her fist at you?'

Harry's face got red. 'She—well, she resented the house being pulled down. And she got the sack, of course. Her husband's been dead two years. They say she got a bit queer after he died.'

'Is she—she isn't—starving?'

Louise's ideas were vague and somewhat melodramatic. Riches prevented you coming into contact with reality.

Harry was outraged. 'Good Lord, Louise, what an idea! I pensioned her off, of course—and handsomely, too! Found her a new cottage and everything.'

Louise asked, bewildered, 'Then why does she mind?'

Harry was frowning, his brows drawn together. 'Oh, how should I know? Craziness! She loved the house.'

'But it was a ruin, wasn't it?'

'Of course it was—crumbling to pieces—roof leaking—more or less unsafe. All the same I suppose it meant something to her. She'd been there a long time. Oh, I don't know! The old devil's cracked, I think.'

Louise said uneasily, 'She—I think she cursed us. Oh, Harry, I wish she hadn't.'

It seemed to Louise that her new home was tainted and poisoned by the malevolent figure of one crazy old woman. When she went out in the car, when she rode, when she walked out with the dogs, there was always the same figure waiting. Crouched down on herself, a battered hat over wisps of iron-grey hair, and the slow muttering of imprecations.

Louise came to believe that Harry was right—the old woman was mad. Nevertheless that did not make things easier. Mrs Murgatroyd never actually came to the house, nor did she use definite threats, nor offer violence. Her squatting figure remained always just outside the gates. To appeal to the police would have been useless and, in any case, Harry Laxton was averse to that course of action. It would, he said, arouse local sympathy for the old brute. He took the matter more easily than Louise did.

'Don't worry about it, darling. She'll get tired of this silly cursing business. Probably she's only trying it on.'

'She isn't, Harry. She—she hates us! I can feel it. She—she's ill-wishing us.'

'She's not a witch, darling, although she may look like one! Don't be morbid about it all.'

Louise was silent. Now that the first excitement of settling in was over, she felt curiously lonely and at a loose end. She had been used to life in London and the Riviera. She had no knowledge of or taste for English country life. She was ignorant of gardening, except for the final act of 'doing the flowers'. She did not really care for dogs. She was bored by such neighbours as she met. She enjoyed riding best, sometimes with Harry, sometimes, when he was busy about the estate, by herself. She hacked through the woods and lanes, enjoying the easy paces of the beautiful horse that Harry had bought for her. Yet even Prince Hal, most sensitive of chestnut steeds, was wont to shy and snort as he carried his mistress past the huddled figure of a malevolent old woman.

One day Louise took her courage in both hands. She was out walking. She had passed Mrs Murgatroyd, pretending not to notice her, but suddenly she swerved back and went right up to her. She said, a little breathlessly, 'What is it? What's the matter? What do you want?'

The old woman blinked at her. She had a cunning, dark gypsy face, with wisps of iron-grey hair, and bleared, suspicious eyes. Louise wondered if she drank.

She spoke in a whining and yet threatening voice. 'What do I want, you ask? What, indeed! That which has been took away from me. Who turned me out of Kingsdean House? I'd lived there, girl and woman, for near on forty years. It was a black deed to turn me out and it's black bad luck it'll bring to you and him!'

Louise said, 'You've got a very nice cottage and—'

She broke off. The old woman's arms flew up. She screamed, 'What's the good of that to me? It's my own place I want and my own fire as I sat beside all them years. And as for you and him, I'm telling you there will be no happiness for you in your new fine house. It's the black sorrow will be upon you! Sorrow and death and my curse. May your fair face rot.'

Louise turned away and broke into a little stumbling run. She thought, I must get away from here! We must sell the house! We must go away.

At the moment, such a solution seemed easy to her. But Harry's utter incomprehension took her back. He exclaimed, 'Leave here? Sell the house? Because of a crazy old woman's threats? You must be mad.'

'No, I'm not. But she—she frightens me, I know something will happen.'

Harry Laxton said grimly, 'Leave Mrs Murgatroyd to me. I'll settle her!'

A friendship had sprung up between Clarice Vane and young Mrs Laxton. The two girls were much of an age, though dissimilar both in character and in tastes. In Clarice's company, Louise found reassurance. Clarice was so self-reliant, so sure of herself. Louise mentioned the matter of Mrs Murgatroyd and her threats, but Clarice seemed to regard the matter as more annoying than frightening.

'It's so stupid, that sort of thing,' she said. 'And really very annoying for you.'

'You know, Clarice, I—I feel quite frightened sometimes. My heart gives the most awful jumps.'

'Nonsense, you mustn't let a silly thing like that get you down. She'll soon tire of it.'

She was silent for a minute or two. Clarice said, 'What's the matter?'

Louise paused for a minute, then her answer came with a rush. 'I hate this place! I hate being here. The woods and this house, and the awful silence at night, and the queer noise owls make. Oh, and the people and everything.'

'The people. What people?'

'The people in the village. Those prying, gossiping old maids.'

Clarice said sharply, 'What have they been saying?'

'I don't know. Nothing particular. But they've got nasty minds. When you've talked to them you feel you wouldn't trust anybody—not anybody at all.'

Clarice said harshly, 'Forget them. They've nothing to do but gossip. And most of the muck they talk they just invent.'

Louise said, 'I wish we'd never come here. But Harry adores it so.' Her voice softened.

Clarice thought, How she adores him. *She said abruptly, 'I must go now.'*

'I'll send you back in the car. Come again soon.'

Clarice nodded. Louise felt comforted by her new friend's visit. Harry was pleased to find her more cheerful and from then on urged her to have Clarice often to the house.

Then one day he said, 'Good news for you, darling.'

'Oh, what?'

'I've fixed the Murgatroyd. She's got a son in America, you know. Well, I've arranged for her to go out and join him. I'll pay her passage.'

'Oh, Harry, how wonderful. I believe I might get to like Kingsdean after all.'

'Get to like it? Why, it's the most wonderful place in the world!'

Louise gave a little shiver. She could not rid herself of her superstitious fear so easily.

If the ladies of St Mary Mead had hoped for the pleasure of imparting information about her husband's past to the bride, this pleasure was denied them by Harry Laxton's own prompt action.

Miss Harmon and Clarice Vane were both in Mr Edge's shop, the one buying mothballs and the other a packet of boracic, when Harry Laxton and his wife came in.

After greeting the two ladies, Harry turned to the counter and was just demanding a toothbrush when he stopped in mid-speech and exclaimed heartily, 'Well, well, just see who's here! Bella, I do declare.'

Mrs Edge, who had hurried out from the back parlour to attend to the congestion of business, beamed back cheerfully at him, showing her big white teeth. She had been a dark, handsome girl and was still a reasonably handsome woman, though she had put on weight, and the lines of her face had coarsened; but her large brown eyes were full of warmth as she answered, 'Bella, it is, Mr Harry, and pleased to see you after all these years.'

Harry turned to his wife. 'Bella's an old flame of mine, Louise,' he said. 'Head-over-heels in love with her, wasn't I, Bella?'

'That's what you say,' said Mrs Edge.

Louise laughed. She said, 'My husband's very happy seeing all his old friends again.'

'Ah,' said Mrs Edge, 'we haven't forgotten you, Mr Harry. Seems like a fairy tale to think of you married and building up a new house instead of that ruined old Kingsdean House.'

'You look very well and blooming,' said Harry, and Mrs Edge laughed and said there was nothing wrong with her and what about that toothbrush?

Clarice, watching the baffled look on Miss Harmon's face, said to herself exultantly, Oh, well done, Harry. You've spiked their guns.

Doctor Haydock said abruptly to his niece, 'What's all this nonsense about old Mrs Murgatroyd hanging about Kingsdean and shaking her fist and cursing the new regime?'

'It isn't nonsense. It's quite true. It's upset Louise a good deal.'

'Tell her she needn't worry—when the Murgatroyds were caretakers they never stopped grumbling about the place—they only stayed because Murgatroyd drank and couldn't get another job.'

'I'll tell her,' said Clarice doubtfully, 'but I don't think she'll believe you. The old woman fairly screams with rage.'

'Always used to be fond of Harry as a boy. I can't understand it.'

Clarice said, 'Oh, well—they'll be rid of her soon. Harry's paying her passage to America.'

Three days later, Louise was thrown from her horse and killed.

Two men in a baker's van were witnesses of the accident. They saw Louise ride out of the gates, saw the old woman spring up and stand in the road waving her arms and shouting, saw the horse start, swerve, and then bolt madly down the road, flinging Louise Laxton over his head.

One of them stood over the unconscious figure, not knowing what to do, while the other rushed to the house to get help.

Harry Laxton came running out, his face ghastly. They took off a door of the van and carried her on it to the house. She died without regaining consciousness and before the doctor arrived.

(End of Doctor Haydock's manuscript.)

When Doctor Haydock arrived the following day, he was pleased to note that there was a pink flush in Miss Marple's cheek and decidedly more animation in her manner.

'Well,' he said, 'what's the verdict?'

'What's the problem, Doctor Haydock?' countered Miss Marple.

'Oh, my dear lady, do I have to tell you that?'

'I suppose,' said Miss Marple, 'that it's the curious conduct of the caretaker. Why did she behave in that very odd way? People do mind being turned out of their old homes. But it wasn't her home. In fact, she used to complain and grumble while she was there. Yes, it certainly looks very fishy. What became of her, by the way?'

'Did a bunk to Liverpool. The accident scared her. Thought she'd wait there for her boat.'

'All very convenient for somebody,' said Miss Marple. 'Yes, I think the "Problem of the Caretaker's Conduct" can be solved easily enough. Bribery, was it not?'

'That's your solution?'

'Well, if it wasn't natural for her to behave in that way, she must have been "putting on an act" as people say, and that means that somebody paid her to do what she did.'

'And you know who that somebody was?'

'Oh, I think so. Money again, I'm afraid. And I've always noticed that gentlemen always tend to admire the same type.'

'Now I'm out of my depth.'

'No, no, it all hangs together. Harry Laxton admired Bella Edge, a dark, vivacious type. Your niece Clarice was the same. But the poor little wife was quite a different type—fair-haired and clinging—not his type at all. So he must have married her for her money. And murdered her for her money, too!'

'You use the word "murder"?'

'Well, he sounds the right type. Attractive to women and quite unscrupulous. I suppose he wanted to keep his wife's money and marry your niece. He may have been seen talking to Mrs Edge. But I don't fancy he was attached to her any more. Though I dare say he made the poor woman think he was, for ends of his own. He soon had her well under his thumb, I fancy.'

'How exactly did he murder her, do you think?'

Miss Marple stared ahead of her for some minutes with dreamy blue eyes.

'It was very well timed—with the baker's van as witness. They could see the old woman and, of course, they'd put down the horse's fright to that. But I should imagine, myself, that an air gun, or perhaps a catapult. Yes, just as the horse came through the gates. The horse bolted, of course, and Mrs Laxton was thrown.'

She paused, frowning.

'The fall might have killed her. But he couldn't be sure of that. And he seems the sort of man who would lay his plans carefully and leave nothing to chance. After all, Mrs Edge could get him something suitable without her husband knowing. Otherwise, why would Harry bother with her? Yes, I think he had some powerful drug handy, that could be administered before you arrived. After all, if a woman is thrown from her horse and has serious injuries and dies without recovering consciousness, well—a doctor wouldn't normally be suspicious, would he? He'd put it down to shock or something.'

Doctor Haydock nodded.

'Why did you suspect?' asked Miss Marple.

'It wasn't any particular cleverness on my part,' said Doctor Haydock. 'It was just the trite, well-known fact that a murderer is so pleased with his cleverness that he doesn't take proper precautions. I was just saying a few consolatory words to the bereaved husband—and feeling damned sorry for the fellow, too—when he flung himself down on the settee to do a bit of play-acting and a hypodermic syringe fell out of his pocket.

'He snatched it up and looked so scared that I began to think. Harry Laxton didn't drug; he was in perfect health;

what was he doing with a hypodermic syringe? I did the autopsy with a view to certain possibilities. I found strophanthin. The rest was easy. There was strophanthin in Laxton's possession, and Bella Edge, questioned by the police, broke down and admitted to having got it for him. And finally old Mrs Murgatroyd confessed that it was Harry Laxton who had put her up to the cursing stunt.'

'And your niece got over it?'

'Yes, she was attracted by the fellow, but it hadn't gone far.'

The doctor picked up his manuscript.

'Full marks to you, Miss Marple—and full marks to me for my prescription. You're looking almost yourself again.'

The Case of the Perfect Maid

'Oh, if you please, madam, could I speak to you a moment?'

It might be thought that this request was in the nature of an absurdity, since Edna, Miss Marple's little maid, was actually speaking to her mistress at the moment.

Recognizing the idiom, however, Miss Marple said promptly, 'Certainly, Edna, come in and shut the door. What is it?'

Obediently shutting the door, Edna advanced into the room, pleated the corner of her apron between her fingers, and swallowed once or twice.

'Yes, Edna?' said Miss Marple encouragingly.

'Oh, please, ma'am, it's my cousin, Gladdie.'

'Dear me,' said Miss Marple, her mind leaping to the worst—and, alas, the most usual conclusion. 'Not—not in trouble?'

Edna hastened to reassure her. 'Oh, no, ma'am, nothing of that kind. Gladdie's not that kind of girl. It's just that she's upset. You see, she's lost her place.'

'Dear me, I am sorry to hear that. She was at Old Hall, wasn't she, with the Miss—Misses—Skinner?'

'Yes, ma'am, that's right, ma'am. And Gladdie's very upset about it—very upset indeed.'

'Gladys has changed places rather often before, though, hasn't she?'

'Oh, yes, ma'am. She's always one for a change, Gladdie is. She never seems to get really settled, if you know what I mean. But she's always been the one to give the notice, you see!'

'And this time it's the other way round?' asked Miss Marple dryly.

'Yes, ma'am, and it's upset Gladdie something awful.'

Miss Marple looked slightly surprised. Her recollection of Gladys, who had occasionally come to drink tea in the kitchen on her 'days out', was a stout, giggling girl of unshakably equable temperament.

Edna went on. 'You see, ma'am, it's the way it happened—the way Miss Skinner looked.'

'How,' enquired Miss Marple patiently, 'did Miss Skinner look?'

This time Edna got well away with her news bulletin.

'Oh, ma'am, it was ever such a shock to Gladdie. You see, one of Miss Emily's brooches was missing, and such a hue and cry for it as never was, and of course nobody likes a thing like that to happen; it's upsetting, ma'am, if you know what I mean. And Gladdie's helped search everywhere, and there was Miss Lavinia saying she was going to the police about it, and then it turned up again, pushed right to the back of a drawer in the dressing-table, and very thankful Gladdie was.

'And the very next day as ever was a plate got broken,

and Miss Lavinia she bounced out right away and told Gladdie to take a month's notice. And what Gladdie feels is it couldn't have been the plate and that Miss Lavinia was just making an excuse of that, and that it must be because of the brooch and they think as she took it and put it back when the police was mentioned, and Gladdie wouldn't do such a thing, not never she wouldn't, and what she feels is as it will get round and tell against her and it's a very serious thing for a girl, as you know, ma'am.'

Miss Marple nodded. Though having no particular liking for the bouncing, self-opinionated Gladys, she was quite sure of the girl's intrinsic honesty and could well imagine that the affair must have upset her.

Edna said wistfully, 'I suppose, ma'am, there isn't anything you could do about it? Gladdie's in ever such a taking.'

'Tell her not to be silly,' said Miss Marple crisply. 'If she didn't take the brooch—which I'm sure she didn't—then she has no cause to be upset.'

'It'll get about,' said Edna dismally.

Miss Marple said, 'I—er—am going up that way this afternoon. I'll have a word with the Misses Skinner.'

'Oh, thank you, madam,' said Edna.

Old Hall was a big Victorian house surrounded by woods and park land. Since it had been proved unlettable and unsaleable as it was, an enterprising speculator had divided it into four flats with a central hot-water system, and the use of 'the grounds' to be held in common by the tenants.

The experiment had been satisfactory. A rich and eccentric old lady and her maid occupied one flat. The old lady had a passion for birds and entertained a feathered gathering to meals every day. A retired Indian judge and his wife rented a second. A very young couple, recently married, occupied the third, and the fourth had been taken only two months ago by two maiden ladies of the name of Skinner. The four sets of tenants were only on the most distant terms with each other, since none of them had anything in common. The landlord had been heard to say that this was an excellent thing. What he dreaded were friendships followed by estrangements and subsequent complaints to him.

Miss Marple was acquainted with all the tenants, though she knew none of them well. The elder Miss Skinner, Miss Lavinia, was what might be termed the working member of the firm. Miss Emily, the younger, spent most of her time in bed suffering from various complaints which, in the opinion of St Mary Mead, were largely imaginary. Only Miss Lavinia believed devoutly in her sister's martyrdom and patience under affliction, and willingly ran errands and trotted up and down to the village for things that 'my sister had suddenly fancied'.

It was the view of St Mary Mead that if Miss Emily suffered half as much as she said she did, she would have sent for Doctor Haydock long ago. But Miss Emily, when this was hinted to her, shut her eyes in a superior way and murmured that her case was not a simple one—the best specialists in London had been baffled by it—and that a wonderful new man had put her on a most revolutionary course of treatment and that she really hoped her health would improve under it. No humdrum GP could possibly understand her case.

'And it's my opinion,' said the outspoken Miss Hartnell, 'that she's very wise not to send for him. Dear Doctor Haydock, in that breezy manner of his, would tell her that there was nothing the matter with her and to get up and not make a fuss! Do her a lot of good!'

Failing such arbitrary treatment, however, Miss Emily continued to lie on sofas, to surround herself with strange little pill boxes, and to reject nearly everything that had been cooked for her and ask for something else—usually something difficult and inconvenient to get.

The door was opened to Miss Marple by 'Gladdie', looking more depressed than Miss Marple had ever thought possible. In the sitting-room (a quarter of the late drawing-room, which had been partitioned into a dining-room, drawing-room, bathroom, and housemaid's cupboard), Miss Lavinia rose to greet Miss Marple.

Lavinia Skinner was a tall, gaunt, bony female of fifty. She had a gruff voice and an abrupt manner.

'Nice to see you,' she said. 'Emily's lying down—feeling low today, poor dear. Hope she'll see you, it would cheer her up, but there are times when she doesn't feel up to seeing anybody. Poor dear, she's wonderfully patient.'

Miss Marple responded politely. Servants were the main topic of conversation in St Mary Mead, so it was not difficult to lead the conversation in that direction.

Miss Marple said she had heard that that nice girl, Gladys Holmes, was leaving.

Miss Lavinia nodded. 'Wednesday week. Broke things, you know. Can't have that.'

Miss Marple sighed and said we all had to put up with things nowadays. It was so difficult to get girls to come to the country. Did Miss Skinner really think it was wise to part with Gladys?

'Know it's difficult to get servants,' admitted Miss Lavinia. 'The Devereuxs haven't got anybody—but then, I don't wonder—always quarrelling, jazz on all night—meals any time—that girl knows nothing of housekeeping. I pity her husband! Then the Larkins have just lost their maid. Of course, what with the judge's Indian temper and his wanting chota hazri, as he calls it, at six in the morning and Mrs Larkin always fussing, I don't wonder at that, either. Mrs Carmichael's Janet is a fixture of course—though in my opinion she's the most disagreeable woman, and absolutely bullies the old lady.'

'Then don't you think you might reconsider your decision about Gladys? She really is a nice girl. I know all her family; very honest and superior.'

Miss Lavinia shook her head.

'I've got my reasons,' she said importantly.

Miss Marple murmured, 'You missed a brooch, I understand—'

'Now, who has been talking? I suppose the girl has. Quite frankly, I'm almost certain she took it. And then got frightened and put it back—but, of course, one can't say anything unless one is sure.' She changed the subject.

'Do come and see Emily, Miss Marple. I'm sure it would do her good.'

Miss Marple followed meekly to where Miss Lavinia knocked on a door, was bidden enter, and ushered her guest into the best room in the flat, most of the light of which was excluded by half-drawn blinds. Miss Emily was lying in bed, apparently enjoying the half-gloom and her own indefinite sufferings.

The dim light showed her to be a thin, indecisive-looking creature, with a good deal of greyish-yellow hair untidily wound around her head and erupting into curls, the whole thing looking like a bird's nest of which no self-respecting bird could be proud. There was a smell in the room of Eau de Cologne, stale biscuits, and camphor.

With half-closed eyes and a thin, weak voice, Emily Skinner explained that this was 'one of her bad days'.

'The worst of ill health is,' said Miss Emily in a melancholy tone, 'that one knows what a burden one is to everyone around one.

'Lavinia is very good to me. Lavvie dear, I do so hate giving trouble but if my hot-water bottle could only be filled in the way I like it—too full it weighs on me so—on the other hand, if it is not sufficiently filled, it gets cold immediately!'

'I'm sorry, dear. Give it to me. I will empty a little out.'

'Perhaps, if you're doing that, it might be refilled. There are no rusks in the house, I suppose—no, no, it doesn't matter. I can do without. Some weak tea and a slice of lemon—no lemons? No, really, I couldn't drink tea without lemon. I think the milk was slightly turned this morning. It has put me against milk in my tea. It doesn't matter. I can do without my tea. Only I do feel so weak. Oysters, they say, are nourishing. I wonder if I could fancy a few? No, no, too much bother to get hold of them so late in the day. I can fast until tomorrow.'

Lavinia left the room murmuring something incoherent about bicycling down to the village.

Miss Emily smiled feebly at her guest and remarked that she did hate giving anyone any trouble.

Miss Marple told Edna that evening that she was afraid her embassy had met with no success.

She was rather troubled to find that rumours as to Gladys's dishonesty were already going around the village.

In the post office, Miss Wetherby tackled her. 'My dear Jane, they gave her a written reference saying she was willing and sober and respectable, but saying nothing about honesty. That seems to me most significant! I hear there was some trouble about a brooch. I think there must be something in it, you know, because one doesn't let a servant go nowadays unless it's something rather grave. They'll find it most difficult to get anyone else. Girls simply will not go to Old Hall. They're nervous coming home on their days out. You'll see, the Skinners won't find anyone else, and then, perhaps, that dreadful hypochondriac sister will have to get up and do something!'

Great was the chagrin of the village when it was made known that the Misses Skinner had engaged, from an agency, a new maid who, by all accounts, was a perfect paragon.

'A three-years' reference recommending her most warmly,

she prefers the country, and actually asks less wages than Gladys. I really feel we have been most fortunate.'

'Well, really,' said Miss Marple, to whom these details were imparted by Miss Lavinia in the fishmonger's shop. 'It does seem too good to be true.'

It then became the opinion of St Mary Mead that the paragon would cry off at the last minute and fail to arrive.

None of these prognostications came true, however, and the village was able to observe the domestic treasure, by name, Mary Higgins, driving through the village in Reed's taxi to Old Hall. It had to be admitted that her appearance was good. A most respectable-looking woman, very neatly dressed.

When Miss Marple next visited Old Hall, on the occasion of recruiting stall-holders for the vicarage fete, Mary Higgins opened the door. She was certainly a most superior-looking maid, at a guess forty years of age, with neat black hair, rosy cheeks, a plump figure discreetly arrayed in black with a white apron and cap—'quite the good, old-fashioned type of servant,' as Miss Marple explained afterwards, and with the proper, inaudible respectful voice, so different from the loud but adenoidal accents of Gladys.

Miss Lavinia was looking far less harassed than usual and, although she regretted that she could not take a stall owing to her preoccupation with her sister, she nevertheless tendered a handsome monetary contribution, and promised to produce a consignment of pen-wipers and babies' socks.

Miss Marple commented on her air of well-being.

'I really feel I owe a great deal to Mary, I am so thankful I had the resolution to get rid of that other girl. Mary is really invaluable. Cooks nicely and waits beautifully and keeps our little flat scrupulously clean—mattresses turned over every day. And she is really wonderful with Emily!'

Miss Marple hastily enquired after Emily.

'Oh, poor dear, she has been very much under the weather lately. She can't help it, of course, but it really makes things a little difficult sometimes. Wanting certain things cooked and then, when they come, saying she can't eat now—and then wanting them again half an hour later and everything spoiled and having to be done again. It makes, of course, a lot of work—but fortunately Mary does not seem to mind at all. She's used to waiting on invalids, she says, and understands them. It is such a comfort.'

'Dear me,' said Miss Marple. 'You are fortunate.'

'Yes, indeed. I really feel Mary has been sent to us as an answer to prayer.'

'She sounds to me,' said Miss Marple, 'almost too good to be true. I should—well, I should be a little careful if I were you.'

Lavinia Skinner failed to perceive the point of this remark. She said, 'Oh! I assure you I do all I can to make her comfortable. I don't know what I should do if she left.'

'I don't expect she'll leave until she's ready to leave,' said Miss Marple and stared very hard at her hostess.

Miss Lavinia said, 'If one has no domestic worries, it takes such a load off one's mind, doesn't it? How is your little Edna shaping?'

'She's doing quite nicely. Not much ahead, of course. Not like your Mary. Still, I do know all about Edna because she's a village girl.'

As she went out into the hall she heard the invalid's voice fretfully raised. 'This compress has been allowed to get quite dry—Doctor Allerton particularly said moisture continually renewed. There, there, leave it. I want a cup of tea and a boiled egg—boiled only three minutes and a half, remember, and send Miss Lavinia to me.'

The efficient Mary emerged from the bedroom and, saying to Lavinia, 'Miss Emily is asking for you, madam,' proceeded to open the door for Miss Marple, helping her into her coat and handing her her umbrella in the most irreproachable fashion.

Miss Marple took the umbrella, dropped it, tried to pick it up, and dropped her bag, which flew open. Mary politely retrieved various odds and ends—a handkerchief, an engagement book, an old-fashioned leather purse, two shillings, three pennies, and a striped piece of peppermint rock.

Miss Marple received the last with some signs of confusion.

'Oh, dear, that must have been Mrs Clement's little boy. He was sucking it, I remember, and he took my bag to play with. He must have put it inside. It's terribly sticky, isn't it?'

'Shall I take it, madam?'

'Oh, would you? Thank you so much.'

Mary stooped to retrieve the last item, a small mirror, upon recovering which Miss Marple exclaimed fervently, 'How lucky, now, that that isn't broken.'

She thereupon departed, Mary standing politely by the door holding a piece of striped rock with a completely expressionless face.

*

For ten days longer St Mary Mead had to endure hearing of the excellencies of Miss Lavinia's and Miss Emily's treasure.

On the eleventh day, the village awoke to its big thrill.

Mary, the paragon, was missing! Her bed had not been slept in, and the front door was found ajar. She had slipped out quietly during the night.

And not Mary alone was missing! Two brooches and five rings of Miss Lavinia's; three rings, a pendant, a bracelet, and four brooches of Miss Emily's were missing, also!

It was the beginning of a chapter of catastrophe.

Young Mrs Devereux had lost her diamonds which she kept in an unlocked drawer and also some valuable furs given to her as a wedding present. The judge and his wife also had had jewellery taken and a certain amount of money. Mrs Carmichael was the greatest sufferer. Not only had she some very valuable jewels but she also kept in the flat a large sum of money which had gone. It had been Janet's evening out, and her mistress was in the habit of walking round the gardens at dusk calling to the birds and scattering crumbs. It seemed clear that Mary, the perfect maid, had had keys to fit all the flats!

There was, it must be confessed, a certain amount of ill-natured pleasure in St Mary Mead. Miss Lavinia had boasted so much of her marvellous Mary.

'And all the time, my dear, just a common thief!'

Interesting revelations followed. Not only had Mary disappeared into the blue, but the agency who had provided her and vouched for her credentials was alarmed to find that the Mary Higgins who had applied to them and whose references they had taken up had, to all intents and purposes, never existed. It was the name of a bona fide servant who had lived with the bona fide sister of a dean, but the real Mary Higgins was existing peacefully in a place in Cornwall.

'Damned clever, the whole thing,' Inspector Slack was forced to admit. 'And, if you ask me, that woman works with a gang. There was a case of much the same kind in Northumberland a year ago. Stuff was never traced, and they never caught her. However, we'll do better than that in Much Benham!'

Inspector Slack was always a confident man.

Nevertheless, weeks passed, and Mary Higgins remained triumphantly at large. In vain Inspector Slack redoubled that energy that so belied his name.

Miss Lavinia remained tearful. Miss Emily was so upset, and felt so alarmed by her condition that she actually sent for Doctor Haydock.

The whole of the village was terribly anxious to know what he thought of Miss Emily's claims to ill health, but naturally could not ask him. Satisfactory data came to hand on the subject, however, through Mr Meek, the chemist's assistant, who was walking out with Clara, Mrs Price-Ridley's maid. It was then known that Doctor Haydock had prescribed a mixture of asafoetida and valerian which, according to Mr Meek, was the stock remedy for malingerers in the army!

Soon afterwards it was learned that Miss Emily, not relishing the medical attention she had had, was declaring that in the state of her health she felt it her duty to be near the specialist in London who understood her case. It was, she said, only fair to Lavinia.

The flat was put up for subletting.

It was a few days after that that Miss Marple, rather pink and flustered, called at the police station in Much Benham and asked for Inspector Slack.

Inspector Slack did not like Miss Marple. But he was aware that the Chief Constable, Colonel Melchett, did not share that opinion. Rather grudgingly, therefore, he received her.

'Good afternoon, Miss Marple, what can I do for you?'

'Oh, dear,' said Miss Marple, 'I'm afraid you're in a hurry.'

'Lots of work on,' said Inspector Slack, 'but I can spare a few moments.'

'Oh dear,' said Miss Marple. 'I hope I shall be able to put what I say properly. So difficult, you know, to explain oneself, don't you think? No, perhaps you don't. But you see, not having been educated in the modern style—just a governess, you know, who taught one the dates of the kings of England and general knowledge—Doctor Brewer—three kinds of diseases of wheat—blight, mildew—now what was the third—was it smut?'

'Do you want to talk about smut?' asked Inspector Slack and then blushed.

'Oh, no, no.' Miss Marple hastily disclaimed any wish to talk about smut. 'Just an illustration, you know. And how needles are made, and all that. Discursive, you know, but not teaching one to keep to the point. Which is what I want to do. It's about Miss Skinner's maid, Gladys, you know.'

'Mary Higgins,' said Inspector Slack.

'Oh, yes, the second maid. But it's Gladys Holmes I mean—rather an impertinent girl and far too pleased with herself but really strictly honest, and it's so important that that should be recognized.'

'No charge against her so far as I know,' said the inspector.

'No, I know there isn't a charge—but that makes it worse. Because, you see, people go on thinking things. Oh, dear—I knew I should explain things badly. What I really mean is that the important thing is to find Mary Higgins.'

'Certainly,' said Inspector Slack. 'Have you any ideas on the subject?'

'Well, as a matter of fact, I have,' said Miss Marple. 'May I ask you a question? Are fingerprints of no use to you?'

'Ah,' said Inspector Slack, 'that's where she was a bit too artful for us. Did most of her work in rubber gloves or housemaid's gloves, it seems. And she'd been careful—wiped off everything in her bedroom and on the sink. Couldn't find a single fingerprint in the place!'

'If you did have her fingerprints, would it help?'

'It might, madam. They may be known at the Yard. This isn't her first job, I'd say!'

Miss Marple nodded brightly. She opened her bag and

extracted a small cardboard box. Inside it, wedged in cotton wool, was a small mirror.

'From my handbag,' said Miss Marple. 'The maid's prints are on it. I think they should be satisfactory—she touched an extremely sticky substance a moment previously.'

Inspector Slack stared. 'Did you get her fingerprints on purpose?'

'Of course.'

'You suspected her then?'

'Well, you know, it did strike me that she was a little too good to be true. I practically told Miss Lavinia so. But she simply wouldn't take the hint! I'm afraid, you know, Inspector, that I don't believe in paragons. Most of us have our faults—and domestic service shows them up very quickly!'

'Well,' said Inspector Slack, recovering his balance, 'I'm obliged to you, I'm sure. We'll send these up to the Yard and see what they have to say.'

He stopped. Miss Marple had put her head a little on one side and was regarding him with a good deal of meaning.

'You wouldn't consider, I suppose, Inspector, looking a little nearer home?'

'What do you mean, Miss Marple?'

'It's very difficult to explain, but when you come across a peculiar thing you notice it. Although, often, peculiar things may be the merest trifles. I've felt that all along, you know; I mean about Gladys and the brooch. She's an honest girl; she didn't take that brooch. Then why did Miss Skinner think she did? Miss Skinner's not a fool; far from it! Why was she so anxious to let a girl go who was a good servant when servants are hard to get? It was peculiar, you know. So I wondered. I wondered a good deal. And I noticed another peculiar thing! Miss Emily's a hypochondriac, but she's the first hypochondriac who hasn't sent for some doctor or other at once. Hypochondriacs love doctors, Miss Emily didn't!'

'What are you suggesting, Miss Marple?'

'Well, I'm suggesting, you know, that Miss Lavinia and Miss Emily are peculiar people. Miss Emily spends nearly all her time in a dark room. And if that hair of hers isn't a wig I—I'll eat my own back switch! And what I say is this—it's perfectly possible for a thin, pale, grey-haired, whining woman to be the same as a black-haired, rosy-cheeked, plump woman. And nobody that I can find ever saw Miss Emily and Mary Higgins at one and the same time.

'Plenty of time to get impressions of all the keys, plenty of time to find out all about the other tenants, and then—get rid of the local girl. Miss Emily takes a brisk walk across country one night and arrives at the station as Mary Higgins next day. And then, at the right moment, Mary Higgins disappears, and off goes the hue and cry after her. I'll tell you where you'll find her, Inspector. On Miss Emily Skinner's sofa! Get her fingerprints if you don't believe me, but you'll find I'm right! A couple of clever thieves, that's what the Skinners are—and no doubt in league with a clever post and rails or fence or whatever you call it. But they won't get away with it this time! I'm not going to have one of our village girls' character for honesty taken away like that! Gladys Holmes is as honest as the day, and everybody's going to know it! Good afternoon!'

Miss Marple had stalked out before Inspector Slack had recovered.

'Whew?' he muttered. 'I wonder if she's right?'

He soon found out that Miss Marple was right again.

Colonel Melchett congratulated Slack on his efficiency, and Miss Marple had Gladys come to tea with Edna and spoke to her seriously on settling down in a good situation when she got one.

Miss Marple Tells a Story

I don't think I've ever told you, my dears—you, Raymond, and you, Joan, about the rather curious little business that happened some years ago now. I don't want to seem *vain* in any way—of course I know that in comparison with you young people I'm not clever at all—Raymond writes those very modern books all about rather unpleasant young men and women—and Joan paints those very remarkable pictures of square people with curious bulges on them—very clever of you, my dear, but as Raymond always says (only quite kindly, because he is the kindest of nephews) I am hopelessly Victorian. I admire Mr Alma-Tadema and Mr Frederic Leighton and I suppose to you they seem hopelessly *vieux jeu*. Now let me see, what was I saying? Oh, yes—that I didn't want to appear vain—but I couldn't help being just a teeny weeny bit pleased with myself, because, just by applying a little common sense, I believe I really did solve a problem that had baffled cleverer heads than mine. Though really I should have thought the whole thing was *obvious* from the beginning . . .

Well, I'll tell you my little story, and if you think I'm inclined to be conceited about it, you must remember that I did at least help a fellow creature who was in very grave distress.

The first I knew of this business was one evening about nine o'clock when Gwen—(you remember Gwen? My little maid with red hair) well—Gwen came in and told me that Mr Petherick and a gentleman had called to see me. Gwen had shown them into the drawing-room—quite rightly. I was sitting in the dining-room because in early spring I think it is so wasteful to have two fires going.

I directed Gwen to bring in the cherry brandy and some glasses and I hurried into the drawing-room. I don't know whether you remember Mr Petherick? He died two years ago, but he had been a friend of mine for many years as well as attending to all my legal business. A very shrewd man and a really clever solicitor. His son does my business for me now—a very nice lad and very up to date—but somehow I don't feel quite the *confidence* I had with Mr Petherick.

I explained to Mr Petherick about the fires and he said at once that he and his friend would come into the dining-room—and then he introduced his friend—a Mr Rhodes. He was a youngish man—not much over forty—and I saw at once there was something very wrong. His manner was most *peculiar*. One might have called it *rude* if one hadn't realized that the poor fellow was suffering from *strain*.

When we were settled in the dining-room and Gwen

had brought the cherry brandy, Mr Petherick explained the reason for his visit.

'Miss Marple,' he said, 'you must forgive an old friend for taking a liberty. What I have come here for is a consultation.'

I couldn't understand at all what he meant, and he went on:

'In a case of illness one likes two points of view—that of the specialist and that of the family physician. It is the fashion to regard the former as of more value, but I am not sure that I agree. The specialist has experience only in his own subject—the family doctor has, perhaps, less knowledge—but a wider experience.'

I knew just what he meant, because a young niece of mine not long before had hurried her child off to a very well-known specialist in skin diseases without consulting her own doctor whom she considered an old dodderer, and the specialist had ordered some very expensive treatment, and later found that all the child was suffering from was a rather unusual form of measles.

I just mention this—though I have a horror of *digressing*—to show that I appreciate Mr Petherick's point—but I still hadn't any idea what he was driving at.

'If Mr Rhodes is ill—' I said, and stopped—because the poor man gave a most dreadful laugh.

He said: 'I expect to die of a broken neck in a few months' time.'

And then it all came out. There had been a case of murder lately in Barnchester—a town about twenty miles away. I'm afraid I hadn't paid much attention to it at the time, because we had been having a lot of excitement in the village about our district nurse, and outside occurrences like an earthquake in India and a murder in Barnchester, although of course far more important really—had given way to our own little local excitements. I'm afraid villages are like that. Still, I *did* remember having read about a woman having been stabbed in a hotel, though I hadn't remembered her name. But now it seemed that this woman had been Mr Rhodes's wife—and as if that wasn't bad enough—he was actually under suspicion of having murdered her himself.

All this Mr Petherick explained to me very clearly, saying that, although the Coronor's jury had brought in a verdict of murder by a person or persons unknown, Mr Rhodes had reason to believe that he would probably be arrested within a day or two, and that he had come to Mr Petherick and placed himself in his hands. Mr Petherick went on to say that they had that afternoon consulted Sir Malcolm Olde, K.C., and that in the event of the case coming to trial Sir Malcolm had been briefed to defend Mr Rhodes.

Sir Malcolm was a young man, Mr Petherick said, very up to date in his methods, and he had indicated a certain line of defence. But with that line of defence Mr Petherick was not entirely satisfied.

'You see, my dear lady,' he said, 'it is tainted with what I call the specialist's point of view. Give Sir Malcolm a case and he sees only one point—the most likely line of defence. But even the best line of defence may ignore completely what is, to my mind, the vital point. It takes no account of what actually happened.'

Then he went on to say some very kind and flattering things about my acumen and judgement and my knowledge of human nature, and asked permission to tell me the story of the case in the hopes that I might be able to suggest some explanation.

I could see that Mr Rhodes was highly sceptical of my being of any use and he was annoyed at being brought here. But Mr Petherick took no notice and proceeded to give me the facts of what occurred on the night of March 8th.

Mr and Mrs Rhodes had been staying at the Crown Hotel in Barnchester. Mrs Rhodes who (so I gathered from Mr Petherick's careful language) was perhaps just a shade of a hypochondriac, had retired to bed immediately after dinner. She and her husband occupied adjoining rooms with a connecting door. Mr Rhodes, who is writing a book on prehistoric flints, settled down to work in the adjoining room. At eleven o'clock he tidied up his papers and prepared to go to bed. Before doing so, he just glanced into his wife's room to make sure that there was nothing she wanted. He discovered the electric light on and his wife lying in bed stabbed through the heart. She had been dead at least an hour—probably longer. The following were the points made. There was another door in Mrs Rhodes's room leading into the corridor. This door was locked and bolted on the inside. The only window in the room was closed and latched. According to Mr Rhodes nobody had passed through the room in which he was sitting except a chambermaid bringing hot-water bottles. The weapon found in the wound was a stiletto dagger which had been lying on Mrs Rhodes's dressing table. She was in the habit of using it as a paper knife. There were no fingerprints on it.

The situation boiled down to this—no one but Mr Rhodes and the chambermaid had entered the victim's room.

I enquired about the chambermaid.

'That was our first line of enquiry,' said Mr Petherick. 'Mary Hill is a local woman. She had been chambermaid at the Crown for ten years. There seems absolutely no reason why she should commit a sudden assault on a guest. She is, in any case, extraordinarily stupid, almost half-witted. Her story has never varied. She brought Mrs Rhodes her hot-water bottle and says the lady was drowsy—just dropping off to sleep. Frankly, I cannot believe, and I am sure no jury would believe, that she committed the crime.'

Mr Petherick went on to mention a few additional details. At the head of the staircase in the Crown Hotel is a kind of miniature lounge where people sometimes sit and have coffee. A passage goes off to the right and the last door in it is the door into the room occupied by Mr Rhodes. The passage then turns sharply to the right again and the first door round the corner is the door into Mrs Rhodes's room. As it happened, both these doors could be seen by witnesses. The first door—that into Mr Rhodes's room, which I will call A, could be seen by four people, two commercial travellers and an elderly married couple who were having coffee. According to them nobody went in or out of door A except Mr Rhodes and the chambermaid. As to the other door in the passage B, there was an electrician at work there and he also swears that nobody entered or left door B except the chambermaid.

It was certainly a very curious and interesting case. On the face of it, it looked as though Mr Rhodes *must* have murdered his wife. But I could see that Mr Petherick was quite convinced of his client's innocence and Mr Petherick was a very shrewd man.

At the inquest Mr Rhodes had told a hesitating and rambling story about some woman who had written threatening letters to his wife. His story, I gathered, had been unconvincing in the extreme. Appealed to by Mr Petherick, he explained himself.

'Frankly,' he said, 'I never believed it. I thought Amy had made most of it up.'

Mrs Rhodes, I gathered, was one of those romantic liars who go through life embroidering everything that happens to them. The amount of adventures that, according to her own account, happened to her in a year was simply incredible. If she slipped on a bit of banana peel it was a case of near escape from death. If a lampshade caught fire she was rescued from a burning building at the hazard of her life. Her husband got into the habit of discounting her statements. Her tale as to some woman whose child she had injured in a motor accident and who had vowed vengeance on her—well—Mr Rhodes had simply not taken any notice of it. The incident had happened before he married his wife and although she had read him letters couched in crazy language, he had suspected her of composing them herself. She had actually done such a thing once or twice before. She was a woman of hysterical tendencies who craved ceaselessly for excitement.

Now, all that seemed to me very natural—indeed, we have a young woman in the village who does much the same thing. The danger with such people is that when anything at all extraordinary really does happen to them, nobody believes they are speaking the truth. It seemed to me that that was what had happened in this case. The police, I gathered, merely believed that Mr Rhodes was making up this unconvincing tale in order to avert suspicion from himself.

I asked if there had been any women staying by themselves in the hotel. It seemed there were two—a Mrs Granby, an Anglo-Indian widow, and a Miss Carruthers, rather a horsey spinster who dropped her g's. Mr Petherick added that the most minute enquiries had failed to elicit anyone who had seen either of them near the scene of the crime and there was nothing to connect either of them with it in any way. I asked him to describe their personal appearance. He said that Mrs Granby had reddish hair rather untidily done, was sallow-faced and about fifty years of age. Her clothes were rather picturesque, being made mostly of native silk, etc. Miss Carruthers was about forty, wore pince-nez, had close-cropped hair like a man and wore mannish coats and skirts.

'Dear me,' I said, 'that makes it very difficult.'

Mr Petherick looked enquiringly at me, but I didn't want to say any more just then, so I asked what Sir Malcolm Olde had said.

Sir Malcolm Olde, it seemed, was going all out for suicide. Mr Petherick said the medical evidence was dead against this, and there was the absence of fingerprints but Sir Malcolm was confident of being able to call conflicting medical testimony and to suggest some way of getting over the fingerprint difficulty. I asked Mr Rhodes what he thought and he said all doctors were fools but he himself couldn't really believe that his wife had killed herself. 'She wasn't that kind of woman,' he said simply—and I believed him. Hysterical people don't usually commit suicide.

I thought a minute and then I asked if the door from Mrs Rhodes's room led straight into the corridor. Mr Rhodes said no—there was a little hallway with a bathroom and lavatory. It was the door from the bedroom to the hallway that was locked and bolted on the inside.

'In that case,' I said, 'the whole thing seems remarkably simple.'

And really, you know, it *did* . . . the simplest thing in the world. And yet no one seemed to have seen it that way.

Both Mr Petherick and Mr Rhodes were staring at me so that I felt quite embarrassed.

'Perhaps,' said Mr Rhodes, 'Miss Marple hasn't quite appreciated the difficulties.'

'Yes,' I said, 'I think I have. There are four possibilities. Either Mrs Rhodes was killed by her husband, or by the chambermaid, or she committed suicide, or she was killed by an outsider whom nobody saw enter or leave.'

'And that's impossible,' Mr Rhodes broke in. 'Nobody could come in or go out through my room without my seeing them, and even if anyone did manage to come in through my wife's room without the electrician seeing them, how the devil could they get out again leaving the door locked and bolted on the inside?'

Mr Petherick looked at me and said: 'Well, Miss Marple?' in an encouraging manner.

'I should like,' I said, 'to ask a question. Mr Rhodes, what did the chambermaid look like?'

He said he wasn't sure—she was tallish, he thought—he didn't remember if she was fair or dark. I turned to Mr Petherick and asked the same question.

He said she was of medium height, had fairish hair and blue eyes and rather a high colour.

Mr Rhodes said: 'You are a better observer than I am, Petherick.'

I ventured to disagree. I then asked Mr Rhodes if he could describe the maid in my house. Neither he nor Mr Petherick could do so.

'Don't you see what that means?' I said. 'You both came here full of your own affairs and the person who let you in was only a *parlourmaid*. The same applies to Mr Rhodes at the hotel. He saw her uniform and her apron. He was engrossed by his work. But Mr Petherick has interviewed the same woman in a different capacity. He has looked at her as a *person*.

'That's what the woman who did the murder counted upon.'

As they still didn't see, I had to explain.

'I think,' I said, 'that this is how it went. The chambermaid came in by door A, passed through Mr Rhodes's room into Mrs Rhodes's room with the hot-water bottle and went out through the hallway into passage B. X—as

I will call our murderess—came in by door B into the little hallway, concealed herself in—well, in a certain apartment, ahem—and waited until the chambermaid had passed out. Then she entered Mrs Rhodes's room, took the stiletto from the dressing table (she had doubtless explored the room earlier in the day), went up to the bed, stabbed the dozing woman, wiped the handle of the stiletto, locked and bolted the door by which she had entered, and then passed out through the room where Mr Rhodes was working.'

Mr Rhodes cried out: 'But I should have *seen* her. The electrician would have seen her go in.'

'No,' I said. 'That's where you're wrong. You wouldn't see her—*not if she were dressed as a chambermaid.*' I let it sink in, then I went on, 'You were engrossed in your work—out of the tail of your eye you saw a chambermaid come in, go into your wife's room, come back and go out. It was the same *dress*—but not the same woman. That's what the people having coffee saw—a chambermaid go in and a chambermaid come out. The electrician did the same. I dare say if a chambermaid were very pretty a gentleman might notice her face—human nature being what it is—but if she were just an ordinary middle-aged woman—well—it would be the chambermaid's *dress* you would see—not the woman herself.'

Mr Rhodes cried: 'Who was she?'

'Well,' I said, 'that is going to be a little difficult. It must be either Mrs Granby or Miss Carruthers. Mrs Granby sounds as though she might wear a wig normally—so she could wear her own hair as a chambermaid. On the other hand, Miss Carruthers with her close-cropped mannish head might easily put on a wig to play her part. I dare say you will find out easily enough which of them it is. Personally, I incline myself to think it will be Miss Carruthers.'

And really, my dears, that is the end of the story. Carruthers was a false name, but she was the woman all right. There was insanity in her family. Mrs Rhodes, who was a most reckless and dangerous driver, had run over her little girl, and it had driven the poor woman off her head. She concealed her madness very cunningly except for writing distinctly insane latters to her intended victim. She had been following her about for some time, and she laid her plans very cleverly. The false hair and maid's dress she posted in a parcel first thing the next morning. When taxed with the truth she broke down and confessed at once. The poor thing is in Broadmoor now. Completely unbalanced of course, but a very cleverly planned crime.

Mr Petherick came to me afterwards and brought me a very nice letter from Mr Rhodes—really, it made me blush. Then my old friend said to me: 'Just one thing—why did you think it was more likely to be Carruthers than Granby? You'd never seen either of them.'

'Well,' I said. 'It was the g's. You said she dropped her g's. Now, that's done by a lot of hunting people in books, but I don't know many people who do it in reality—and certainly no one under sixty. You said this woman was forty. Those dropped g's sounded to me like a woman who was playing a part and over-doing it.'

I shan't tell you what Mr Petherick said to that—but he

was very complimentary—and I really couldn't help feeling just a teeny weeny bit pleased with myself.

And it's extraordinary how things turn out for the best in this world. Mr Rhodes has married again—such a nice, sensible girl—and they've got a dear little baby and—what do you think?—they asked me to be godmother. Wasn't it nice of them?

Now I do hope you don't think I've been running on too long . . .

The Dressmaker's Doll

The doll lay in the big velvet-covered chair. There was not much light in the room; the London skies were dark. In the gentle, greyish-green gloom, the sage-green coverings and the curtains and the rugs all blended with each other. The doll blended, too. She lay long and limp and sprawled in her green-velvet clothes and her velvet cap and the painted mask of her face. She was not a doll as children understand dolls. She was the Puppet Doll, the whim of Rich Women, the doll who lolls beside the telephone, or among the cushions of the divan. She sprawled there, eternally limp and yet strangely alive. She looked a decadent product of the twentieth century.

Sybil Fox, hurrying in with some patterns and a sketch, looked at the doll with a faint feeling of surprise and bewilderment. She wondered—but whatever she wondered did not get to the front of her mind. Instead, she thought to herself, 'Now, what's happened to the pattern of the blue velvet? Wherever have I put it? I'm sure I had it here just now.' She went out on the landing and called up to the workroom.

'Elspeth, Elspeth, have you the blue pattern up there? Mrs Fellows-Brown will be here any minute now.'

She went in again, switching on the lights. Again she glanced at the doll. 'Now where on earth—ah, there it is.' She picked the pattern up from where it had fallen from her hand. There was the usual creak outside on the landing as the elevator came to a halt and in a minute or two Mrs Fellows-Brown, accompanied by her Pekinese, came puffing into the room rather like a fussy local train arriving at a wayside station.

'It's going to pour,' she said, 'simply *pour*!'

She threw off her gloves and a fur. Alicia Coombe came in. She didn't always come in nowadays, only when special customers arrived, and Mrs Fellows-Brown was such a customer.

Elspeth, the forewoman of the workroom, came down with the frock and Sybil pulled it over Mrs Fellows-Brown's head.

'There,' she said. 'It really does suit you. It's a lovely colour, isn't it?'

Alicia Coombe sat back a little in her chair, studying it.

'Yes,' she said, 'I think it's good. Yes, it's definitely a success.'

Mrs Fellows-Brown turned sideways and looked in the mirror.

'I must say,' she said, 'your clothes do *do* something to my behind.'

'You're much thinner than you were three months ago,' Sybil assured her.

'I'm really not,' said Mrs Fellows-Brown, 'though I must say I *look* it in this. There's something about the way you cut, it really does minimize my behind. I almost look as though I hadn't got one—I mean only the usual kind that most people have.' She sighed and gingerly smoothed the troublesome portion of her anatomy. 'It's always been a bit of a trial to me,' she said. 'Of course, for years I could pull it in, you know, by sticking out my front. Well, I can't do that any longer because I've got a stomach now as well as a behind. And I mean—well, you can't pull it in both ways, can you?'

Alicia Coombe said, 'You should see some of my customers!'

Mrs Fellows-Brown experimented to and fro.

'A stomach is worse than a behind,' she said. 'It shows more. Or perhaps you think it does, because, I mean, when you're talking to people you're facing them and that's the moment they can't see your behind but they can notice your stomach. Anyway, I've made it a rule to pull in my stomach and let my behind look after itself.' She craned her neck round still farther, then said suddenly, 'Oh, that doll of yours! She gives me the creeps. How long have you had her?'

Sybil glanced uncertainly at Alicia Coombe, who looked puzzled but vaguely distressed.

'I don't know exactly . . . some time I think—I never *can* remember things. It's awful nowadays—I simply *cannot* remember. Sybil, how long have we had her?'

Sybil said shortly, 'I don't know.'

'Well,' said Mrs Fellows-Brown, 'she gives *me* the creeps. Uncanny! She looks, you know, as though she was watching us all, and perhaps laughing in that velvet sleeve of hers. I'd get rid of her if I were you.' She gave a little shiver, then she plunged once more into dress-making details. Should she or should she not have the sleeves an inch shorter? And what about the length? When all these important points were settled satisfactorily, Mrs Fellows-Brown resumed her own garments and prepared to leave. As she passed the doll, she turned her head again.

'No,' she said, 'I *don't* like that doll. She looks too much as though she *belonged* here. It isn't healthy.'

'Now what did she mean by that?' demanded Sybil, as Mrs Fellows-Brown departed down the stairs.

Before Alicia Coombe could answer, Mrs Fellows-Brown returned, poking her head round the door.

'Good gracious, I forgot all about Fou-Ling. Where are you, ducksie? Well, I never!'

She stared and the other two women stared, too. The Pekinese was sitting by the green-velvet chair, staring up at the limp doll sprawled on it. There was no expression, either of pleasure or resentment, on his small, pop-eyed face. He was merely looking.

'Come along, mum's darling,' said Mrs Fellows-Brown.

Mum's darling paid no attention whatever.

'He gets more disobedient every day,' said Mrs Fellows-Brown, with the air of one cataloguing a virtue. 'Come *on*, Fou-Ling. Dindins. Luffly liver.'

Fou-Ling turned his head about an inch and a half towards his mistress, then with disdain resumed his appraisal of the doll.

'She's certainly made an impression on him,' said Mrs Fellows-Brown. 'I don't think he's ever noticed her before. *I* haven't either. Was she here last time I came?'

The other two women looked at each other. Sybil now

had a frown on her face, and Alicia Coombe said, wrinkling up her forehead, 'I told you—I simply can't remember anything nowadays. How long *have* we had her, Sybil?'

'Where did she come from?' demanded Mrs Fellows-Brown. 'Did you buy her?'

'Oh no.' Somehow Alicia Coombe was shocked at the idea. 'Oh *no*. I suppose—I suppose someone gave her to me.' She shook her head. 'Maddening!' she exclaimed. 'Absolutely maddening, when everything goes out of your head the very moment after it's happened.'

'Now don't be stupid, Fou-Ling,' said Mrs Fellows-Brown sharply. 'Come on. I'll have to pick you up.'

She picked him up. Fou-Ling uttered a short bark of agonized protest. They went out of the room with Fou-Ling's pop-eyed face turned over his fluffy shoulder, still staring with enormous attention at the doll on the chair . . .

'That there doll,' said Mrs Groves, 'fair gives me the creeps, it does.'

Mrs Groves was the cleaner. She had just finished a crab-like progress backwards along the floor. Now she was standing up and working slowly round the room with a duster.

'Funny thing,' said Mrs Groves, 'never noticed it really until yesterday. And then it hit me all of a sudden, as you might say.'

'You don't like it?' asked Sybil.

'I tell you, Mrs Fox, it gives me the creeps,' said the cleaning woman. 'It ain't natural, if you know what I mean. All those long hanging legs and the way she's slouched down there and the cunning look she has in her eye. It doesn't look healthy, that's what I say.'

'You've never said anything about her before,' said Sybil.

'I tell you, I never noticed her—not till this morning . . . Of course I know she's been here some time but—' She stopped and a puzzled expression flitted across her face. 'Sort of thing you might dream of at night,' she said, and gathering up various cleaning implements she departed from the fitting-room and walked across the landing to the room on the other side.

Sybil stared at the relaxed doll. An expression of bewilderment was growing on her face. Alicia Coombe entered and Sybil turned sharply.

'Miss Coombe, how long *have* you had this creature?'

'What, the doll? My dear, you know I can't remember things. Yesterday—why, it's too silly!—I was going out to that lecture and I hadn't gone halfway down the street when I suddenly found I couldn't remember where I was going. I thought and I thought. Finally I told myself it *must* be Fortnums. I knew there was something I wanted to get at Fortnums. Well, you won't believe me, it wasn't till I actually got home and was having some tea that I remembered about the lecture. Of course, I've always heard that people go gaga as they get on in life, but it's happening to me much too fast. I've forgotten now where I've put my handbag—and my spectacles, too. Where did I put those spectacles? I had them just now—I was reading something in *The Times*.'

'The spectacles are on the mantelpiece here,' said Sybil, handing them to her. 'How did you get the doll? Who gave her to you?'

'That's a blank, too,' said Alicia Coombe. '*Somebody*

gave her to me or sent her to me, I suppose . . . However, she does seem to match the room very well, doesn't she?'

'Rather too well, I think,' said Sybil. 'Funny thing is, *I* can't remember when I first noticed her here.'

'Now don't you get the same way as I am,' Alicia Coombe admonished her. 'After all, you're young still.'

'But really, Miss Coombe, I don't remember. I mean, I looked at her yesterday and thought there was something—well, Mrs Groves is quite right—something creepy about her. And then I thought I'd already thought so, and then I tried to remember when I first thought so, and—well, I just couldn't remember anything! In a way, it was as if I'd never seen her before—only it didn't feel like that. It felt as though she'd been here a long time but I'd only just noticed her.'

'Perhaps she flew in through the window one day on a broomstick,' said Alicia Coombe. 'Anyway, she belongs here now all right.' She looked round. 'You could hardly imagine the room without her, could you?'

'No,' said Sybil, with a slight shiver, 'but I rather wish I could.'

'Could what?'

'Imagine the room without her.'

'Are we all going barmy about this doll?' demanded Alicia Coombe impatiently. 'What's wrong with the poor thing? Looks like a decayed cabbage to me, but perhaps,' she added, 'that's because I haven't got spectacles on.' She put them on her nose and looked firmly at the doll. 'Yes,' she said, 'I see what you mean. She *is* a little creepy . . . Sad-looking but—well, sly and rather determined, too.'

'Funny,' said Sybil, 'Mrs Fellows-Brown taking such a violent dislike to her.'

'She's one who never minds speaking her mind,' said Alicia Coombe.

'But it's odd,' persisted Sybil, 'that this doll should make such an impression on her.'

'Well, people do take dislikes very suddenly sometimes.'

'Perhaps,' said Sybil with a little laugh, 'that doll never *was* here until yesterday . . . Perhaps she just—flew in through the window, as you say, and settled herself here.'

'No,' said Alicia Coombe, 'I'm sure she's been here some time. Perhaps she only became visible yesterday.'

'That's what I feel, too,' said Sybil, 'that she's been here some time . . . but all the same I *don't* remember really seeing her till yesterday.'

'Now, dear,' said Alicia Coombe briskly, 'do stop it. You're making me feel quite peculiar with shivers running up and down my spine. You're not going to work up a great deal of supernatural hoo-hah about that creature, are you?' She picked up the doll, shook it out, rearranged its shoulders, and sat it down again on another chair. Immediately the doll flopped slightly and relaxed.

'It's not a bit lifelike,' said Alicia Coombe, staring at the doll. 'And yet, in a funny way, she does seem alive, doesn't she?'

'Oo, it did give me a turn,' said Mrs Groves, as she went round the showroom, dusting. 'Such a turn as I hardly like to go into the fitting-room any more.'

'What's given you a turn?' demanded Miss Coombe who was sitting at a writing-table in the corner, busy with various accounts. 'This woman,' she added more for her own benefit than that of Mrs Groves, 'thinks she can have two evening dresses, three cocktail dresses, and a suit every year without ever paying me a penny for them! Really, some people!'

'It's that doll,' said Mrs Groves.

'What, our doll again?'

'Yes, sitting up there at the desk, like a human. Oo, it didn't half give me a turn!'

'What are you talking about?'

Alicia Coombe got up, strode across the room, across the landing outside, and into the room opposite—the fitting-room. There was a small Sheraton desk in one corner of it, and there, sitting in a chair drawn up to it, her long floppy arms on the desk, sat the doll.

'Sombody seems to have been having fun,' said Alicia Coombe. 'Fancy sitting her up like that. Really, she looks quite natural.'

Sybil Fox came down the stairs at this moment, carrying a dress that was to be tried on that morning.

'Come here, Sybil. Look at our doll sitting at my private desk and writing letters now.'

The two women looked.

'Really,' said Alicia Coombe, 'it's too ridiculous! I wonder who propped her up there. Did you?'

'No, I didn't,' said Sybil. 'It must have been one of the girls from upstairs.'

'A silly sort of joke, really,' said Alicia Coombe. She picked up the doll from the desk and threw her back on the sofa.

Sybil laid the dress over a chair carefully, then she went out and up the stairs to the workroom.

'You know the doll,' she said, 'the velvet doll in Miss Coombe's room downstairs—in the fitting room?'

The forewoman and three of the girls looked up.

'Yes, miss, of course we know.'

'Who sat her up at the desk this morning for a joke?'

The three girls looked at her, then Elspeth, the forewoman, said, 'Sat her up at the desk? *I* didn't.'

'Nor did I,' said one of the girls. 'Did you, Marlene?' Marlene shook her head.

'This your bit of fun, Elspeth?'

'No, indeed,' said Elspeth, a stern woman who looked as though her mouth should always be filled with pins. 'I've more to do than going about playing with dolls and sitting them up at desks.'

'Look here,' said Sybil, and to her surprise her voice shook slightly. 'It was—it was quite a good joke, only I'd just like to know who did it.'

The three girls bristled.

'We've told you, Mrs Fox. None of us did it, did we, Marlene?'

'I didn't,' said Marlene, 'and if Nellie and Margaret say they didn't, well then, none of us did.'

'You've heard what *I* had to say,' said Elspeth. 'What's this all about anyway, Mrs Fox?'

'Perhaps it was Mrs Groves?' said Marlene.

Sybil shook her head. 'It wouldn't be Mrs Groves. It gave *her* quite a turn.'

'I'll come down and see for myself,' said Elspeth.

'She's not there now,' said Sybil. 'Miss Coombe took her away from the desk and threw her back on the sofa. Well—' she paused—'what I mean is, someone must have stuck her up there in the chair at the writing-desk—thinking it was funny. I suppose. And—and I don't see why they won't say so.'

'I've told you twice, Mrs Fox,' said Margaret. 'I don't see why you should go on accusing us of telling lies. None of us would do a silly thing like that.'

'I'm sorry,' said Sybil, 'I didn't mean to upset you. But—but who else could possibly have done it?'

'Perhaps she got up and walked there herself,' said Marlene, and giggled.

For some reason Sybil didn't like the suggestion.

'Oh, it's all a lot of nonsense, anyway,' she said, and went down the stairs again.

Alicia Coombe was humming quite cheerfully. She looked round the room.

'I've lost my spectacles again,' she said, 'but it doesn't really matter. I don't want to see anything this moment. The trouble is, of course, when you're as blind as I am, that when you have lost your spectacles, unless you've got another pair to put on and find them with, well, then you can't find them because you can't see to find them.'

'I'll look round for you,' said Sybil. 'You had them just now.'

'I went into the other room when you went upstairs. I expect I took them back in there.'

She went across to the other room.

'It's such a bother,' said Alicia Coombe. 'I want to get

on with these accounts. How can I if I haven't my spectacles?'

'I'll go up and get your second pair from the bedroom,' said Sybil.

'I haven't got a second pair at present,' said Alicia Coombe.

'Why, what's happened to them?'

'Well, I think I left them yesterday when I was out at lunch. I've rung up there, and I've rung up the two shops I went into, too.'

'Oh, dear,' said Sybil, 'you'll have to get *three* pairs, I suppose.'

'If I had three pairs of spectacles,' said Alicia Coombe, 'I should spend my whole life looking for one or the other of them. I really think it's best to have only *one*. Then you've *got* to look till you find it.'

'Well, they must be somewhere,' said Sybil. 'You haven't been out of these two rooms. They're certainly not here, so you must have laid them down in the fitting-room.'

She went back, walking round, looking quite closely. Finally, as a last idea, she took up the doll from the sofa.

'I've got them,' she called.

'Oh, where were they, Sybil?'

'Under our precious doll. I suppose you must have thrown them down when you put her back on the sofa.'

'I didn't. I'm sure I didn't.'

'Oh,' said Sybil with exasperation. 'Then I suppose the doll took them and was hiding them from you!'

'Really, you know,' said Alicia, looking thoughtfully at the doll, 'I wouldn't put it past her. She looks very intelligent, don't you think, Sybil?'

'I don't think I like her face,' said Sybil. 'She looks as though she knew something that we didn't.'

'You don't think she looks sort of sad and sweet?' said Alicia Coombe pleadingly, but without conviction.

'I don't think she's in the least sweet,' said Sybil.

'No . . . perhaps you're right . . . Oh, well, let's get on with things. Lady Lee will be here in another ten minutes. I just want to get these invoices done and posted.'

'Mrs Fox. Mrs Fox?'

'Yes, Margaret?' said Sybil. 'What is it?'

Sybil was busy leaning over a table, cutting a piece of satin material.

'Oh, Mrs Fox, it's that doll again. I took down the brown dress like you said, and there's that doll sitting up at the desk again. And it wasn't me—it wasn't any of us. Please, Mrs Fox, we really wouldn't do such a thing.'

Sybil's scissors slid a little.

'There,' she said angrily, 'look what you've made me do. Oh, well, it'll be all right, I suppose. Now, what's this about the doll?'

'She's sitting at the desk again.'

Sybil went down and walked into the fitting-room. The doll was sitting at the desk exactly as she had sat there before.

'You're very determined, aren't you?' said Sybil, speaking to the doll.

She picked her up unceremoniously and put her back on the sofa.

'That's your place, my girl,' she said. 'You stay there.'

She walked across to the other room.

'Miss Coombe.'

'Yes, Sybil?'

'Somebody *is* having a game with us, you know. That doll was sitting at the desk again.'

'Who do you think it is?'

'It must be one of those three upstairs,' said Sybil. 'Thinks it's funny, I suppose. Of course they all swear to high heaven it wasn't them.'

'Who do you think it is—Margaret?'

'No, I don't think it's Margaret. She looked quite queer when she came in and told me. I expect it's that giggling Marlene.'

'Anyway, it's a very silly thing to do.'

'Of course it is—idiotic,' said Sybil. 'However,' she added grimly, 'I'm going to put a stop to it.'

'What are you going to do?'

'You'll see,' said Sybil.

That night when she left, she locked the fitting-room from the outside.

'I'm locking this door,' she said, 'and I'm taking the key with me.'

'Oh, I see,' said Alicia Coombe, with a faint air of amusement. 'You're beginning to think it's me, are you? You think I'm so absent-minded that I go in there and think I'll write at the desk, but instead I pick the doll up and put her there to write for me. Is that the idea? And then I forget all about it?'

'Well, it's a possibility,' Sybil admitted. 'Anyway, I'm

going to be quite sure that no silly practical joke is played tonight.'

The following morning, her lips set grimly, the first thing Sybil did on arrival was to unlock the door of the fitting-room and march in. Mrs Groves, with an aggrieved expression and mop and duster in hand, had been waiting on the landing.

'*Now* we'll see!' said Sybil.

Then she drew back with a slight gasp.

The doll was sitting at the desk.

'Coo!' said Mrs Groves behind her. 'It's uncanny! That's what it is. Oh, there, Mrs Fox, you look quite pale, as though you've come over queer. You need a little drop of something. Has Miss Coombe got a drop upstairs, do you know?'

'I'm quite all right,' said Sybil.

She walked over to the doll, lifted her carefully, and crossed the room with her.

'Somebody's been playing a trick on you again,' said Mrs Groves.

'I don't see how they could have played a trick on me this time,' said Sybil slowly. 'I locked that door last night. You know yourself that no one could get in.'

'Somebody's got another key, maybe,' said Mrs Groves helpfully.

'I don't think so,' said Sybil. 'We've never bothered to lock this door before. It's one of those old-fashioned keys and there's only one of them.'

'Perhaps the other key fits it—the one to the door opposite.'

In due course they tried all the keys in the shop, but none fitted the door of the fitting-room.

'It *is* odd, Miss Coombe,' said Sybil later, as they were having lunch together.

Alicia Coombe was looking rather pleased.

'My dear,' she said. 'I think it's simply extraordinary. I think we ought to write to the psychical research people about it. You know, they might send an investigator—a medium or someone—to see if there's anything peculiar about the room.'

'You don't seem to mind at all,' said Sybil.

'Well, I rather enjoy it in a way,' said Alicia Coombe. 'I mean, at my age, it's rather fun when things happen! All the same—no,' she added thoughtfully. 'I don't think I do quite like it. I mean, that doll's getting rather above herself, isn't she?'

On that evening Sybil and Alicia Coombe locked the door once more on the outside.

'I still think,' said Sybil, 'that somebody might be playing a practical joke, though, really, I don't see why . . .'

'Do you think she'll be at the desk again tomorrow morning?' demanded Alicia.

'Yes,' said Sybil, 'I do.'

But they were wrong. The doll was not at the desk. Instead, she was on the window sill, looking out into the street. And again there was an extraordinary naturalness about her position.

'It's all frightfully silly, isn't it?' said Alicia Coombe, as they were snatching a quick cup of tea that afternoon. By common consent they were not having it in the fitting-room, as they usually did, but in Alicia Coombe's own room opposite.

'Silly in what way?'

'Well, I mean, there's nothing you can get hold of. Just a doll that's always in a different place.'

As day followed day it seemed a more and more apt observation. It was not only at night that the doll now moved. At any moment when they came into the fitting-room, after they had been absent even a few minutes, they might find the doll in a different place. They could have left her on the sofa and find her on a chair. Then she'd be on a different chair. Sometimes she'd be in the window seat, sometimes at the desk again.

'She just moves about as she likes,' said Alicia Coombe. 'And I think, Sybil, I *think* it's amusing her.'

The two women stood looking down at the inert sprawling figure in its limp, soft velvet, with its painted silk face.

'Some old bits of velvet and silk and a lick of paint, that's all it is,' said Alicia Coombe. Her voice was strained. 'I suppose, you know, we could—er—we could dispose of her.'

'What do you mean, dispose of her?' asked Sybil. Her voice sounded almost shocked.

'Well,' said Alicia Coombe, 'we could put her in the fire, if there was a fire. Burn her, I mean, like a witch . . . Or of course,' she added matter-of-factly, 'we could just put her in the dustbin.'

'I don't think that would do,' said Sybil. 'Somebody would probably take her out of the dustbin and bring her back to us.'

'Or we could send her somewhere,' said Alicia Coombe. 'You know, to one of those societies who are always writing and asking for something—for a sale or a bazaar. I think that's the best idea.'

'I don't know . . .' said Sybil. 'I'd be almost afraid to do that.'

'Afraid?'

'Well, I think she'd come back,' said Sybil.

'You mean, she'd come back *here*?'

'Yes.'

'Like a homing pigeon?'

'Yes, that's what I mean.'

'I suppose we're not going off our heads, are we?' said Alicia Coombe. 'Perhaps I've really gone gaga and perhaps you're just humouring me, is that it?'

'No,' said Sybil. 'But I've got a nasty frightening feeling—a horrid feeling that she's too strong for us.'

'What? That mess of rags?'

'Yes, that horrible limp mess of rags. Because, you see, she's so determined.'

'Determined?'

'To have her own way! I mean, this is *her* room now!'

'Yes,' said Alicia Coombe, looking round, 'it is, isn't it? Of course, it always was, when you come to think of it—the colours and everything . . . I thought she fitted in here, but it's the room that fits her. I must say,' added the dressmaker, with a touch of briskness in her voice, 'it's rather absurd when a doll comes and takes possession of things like this. You know, Mrs Groves won't come in here any longer and clean.'

'Does she say she's frightened of the doll?'

'No. She just makes excuses of some kind or other.' Then Alicia added with a hint of panic, 'What are we going to do, Sybil? It's getting me down, you know. I haven't been able to design anything for weeks.'

'I can't keep my mind on cutting out properly,' Sybil confessed. 'I make all sorts of silly mistakes. Perhaps,' she said uncertainly, 'your idea of writing to the psychical research people might do some good.'

'Just make us look like a couple of fools,' said Alicia Coombe. 'I didn't seriously mean it. No, I suppose we'll just have to go on until—'

'Until what?'

'Oh, I don't know,' said Alicia, and she laughed uncertainly.

On the following day Sybil, when she arrived, found the door of the fitting-room locked.

'Miss Coombe, have you got the key? Did you lock this last night?'

'Yes,' said Alicia Coombe, 'I locked it and it's going to stay locked.'

'What do you mean?'

'I just mean I've given up the room. The doll can have it. We don't need two rooms. We can fit in here.'

'But it's your own private sitting-room.'

'Well, I don't want it any more. I've got a very nice bedroom. I can make a bed-sitting room out of that, can't I?'

'Do you mean you're really not going into that fitting-room ever again?' said Sybil incredulously.

'That's exactly what I mean.'

'But—what about cleaning? It'll get in a terrible state.'

'Let it!' said Alicia Coombe. 'If this place is suffering from some kind of possession by a doll, all right—let her keep possession. And clean the room herself.' And she added, 'She hates us, you know.'

'What do you mean?' said Sybil. 'The doll *hates* us?'

'Yes,' said Alicia. 'Didn't you know? You must have known. You must have seen it when you looked at her.'

'Yes,' said Sybil thoughtfully, 'I suppose I did. I suppose I felt that all along—that she hated us and wanted to get us out of there.'

'She's a malicious little thing,' said Alicia Coombe. 'Anyway, she ought to be satisfied now.'

Things went on rather more peacefully after that. Alicia Coombe announced to her staff that she was giving up the use of the fitting-room for the present—it made too many rooms to dust and clean, she explained.

But it hardly helped her to overhear one of the work girls saying to another on the evening of the same day, 'She really is batty, Miss Coombe is now. I always thought she was a bit queer—the way she lost things and forgot things. But it's really beyond anything now, isn't it? She's got a sort of thing about that doll downstairs.'

'Ooo, you don't think she'll go really bats, do you?' said the other girl. 'That she might knife us or something?'

They passed, chattering, and Alicia sat up indignantly in her chair. Going bats indeed! Then she added ruefully, to herself, 'I suppose, if it wasn't for Sybil, I should think myself that I was going bats. But with me and Sybil and

Mrs Groves too, well, it does look as though there was *something* in it. But what I don't see is, how is it going to end?'

Three weeks later, Sybil said to Alicia Coombe, 'We've got to go into that room *sometimes*.'

'Why?'

'Well, I mean, it must be in a filthy state. Moths will be getting into things, and all that. We ought just to dust and sweep it and then lock it up again.'

'I'd much rather keep it shut up and not go back in there,' said Alicia Coombe.

Sybil said, 'Really, you know, you're even more superstitious than I am.'

'I suppose I am,' said Alicia Coombe. 'I was much more ready to believe in all this than you were, but to begin with, you know—I—well, I found it exciting in an odd sort of way. I don't know. I'm just scared, and I'd rather not go into that room again.'

'Well, I want to,' said Sybil, 'and I'm going to.'

'You know what's the matter with you?' said Alicia Coombe. 'You're simply curious, that's all.'

'All right, then I'm curious. I want to see what the doll's done.'

'I still think it's much better to leave her alone,' said Alicia. 'Now we've got out of that room, she's satisfied. You'd better leave her satisfied.' She gave an exasperated sigh. 'What nonsense we are talking!'

'Yes. I know we're talking nonsense, but if you tell me of any way of *not* talking nonsense—come on, now, give me the key.'

'All right, all right.'

'I believe you're afraid I'll let her out or something. I should think she was the kind that could pass through doors or windows.'

Sybil unlocked the door and went in.

'How terribly odd,' she said.

'What's odd?' said Alicia Coombe, peering over her shoulder.

'The room hardly seems dusty at all, does it? You'd think, after being shut up all this time—'

'Yes, it is odd.'

'There she is,' said Sybil.

The doll was on the sofa. She was not lying in her usual limp position. She was sitting upright, a cushion behind her back. She had the air of the mistress of the house, waiting to receive people.

'Well,' said Alicia Coombe, 'she seems at home all right, doesn't she? I almost feel I ought to apologize for coming in.'

'Let's go,' said Sybil.

She backed out, pulling the door to, and locked it again.

The two women gazed at each other.

'I wish I knew,' said Alicia Coombe, 'why it scares us so much . . .'

'My goodness, who wouldn't be scared?'

'Well, I mean, what *happens*, after all? It's nothing really—just a kind of puppet that gets moved around the room. I expect it isn't the puppet itself—it's a poltergeist.'

'Now that *is* a good idea.'

'Yes, but I don't really believe it. I think it's—it's that doll.'

'Are you *sure* you don't know where she really came from?'

'I haven't the faintest idea,' said Alicia. 'And the more I think of it the more I'm perfectly certain that I didn't buy her, and that nobody gave her to me. I think she—well, she just came.'

'Do you think she'll—ever go?'

'Really,' said Alicia, 'I don't see why she should . . . She's got all she wants.'

But it seemed that the doll had not got all she wanted. The next day, when Sybil went into the showroom, she drew in her breath with a sudden gasp. Then she called up the stairs.

'Miss Coombe, Miss Coombe, come down here.'

'What's the matter?'

Alicia Coombe, who had got up late, came down the stairs, hobbling a little precariously for she had rheumatism in her right knee.

'What is the matter with you, Sybil?'

'Look. Look what's happened now.'

They stood in the doorway of the showroom. Sitting on a sofa, sprawled easily over the arm of it, was the doll.

'She's got out,' said Sybil, '*She's got out of that room!* She wants this room as well.'

Alicia Coombe sat down by the door. 'In the end,' she said, 'I suppose she'll want the whole shop.'

'She might,' said Sybil.

'You nasty, sly, malicious brute,' said Alicia, addressing the doll. 'Why do you want to come and pester us so? We don't want you.'

It seemed to her, and to Sybil too, that the doll moved very slightly. It was as though its limbs relaxed still further. A long limp arm was lying on the arm of the sofa and the half-hidden face looked as if it were peering from under the arm. And it was a sly, malicious look.

'Horrible creature,' said Alicia. 'I can't bear it! I can't bear it any longer.'

Suddenly, taking Sybil completely by surprise, she dashed across the room, picked up the doll, ran to the window, opened it, and flung the doll out into the street. There was a gasp and a half cry of fear from Sybil.

'Oh, Alicia, you shouldn't have done that! I'm sure you shouldn't have done that!'

'I had to do something,' said Alicia Coombe. 'I just couldn't stand it any more.'

Sybil joined her at the window. Down below on the pavement the doll lay, loose-limbed, face down.

'You've *killed* her,' said Sybil.

'Don't be absurd . . . How can I kill something that's made of velvet and silk, bits and pieces? It's not real.'

'It's horribly real,' said Sybil.

Alicia caught her breath.

'Good heavens. That child—'

A small ragged girl was standing over the doll on the pavement. She looked up and down the street—a street that was not unduly crowded at this time of the morning though there was some automobile traffic; then, as though satisfied, the child bent, picked up the doll, and ran across the street.

'Stop, stop!' called Alicia.

She turned to Sybil.

'That child mustn't take the doll. She *mustn't*! That doll is dangerous—it's evil. We've got to stop her.'

It was not they who stopped her. It was the traffic. At that moment three taxis came down one way and two tradesmen's vans in the other direction. The child was marooned on an island in the middle of the road. Sybil rushed down the stairs, Alicia Coombe following her. Dodging between a tradesman's van and a private car, Sybil, with Alicia Coombe directly behind her, arrived on the island before the child could get through the traffic on the opposite side.

'You can't take that doll,' said Alicia Coombe. 'Give her back to me.'

The child looked at her. She was a skinny little girl about eight years old, with a slight squint. Her face was defiant.

'Why should I give 'er to you?' she said. 'Pitched her out of the window, you did—I saw you. If you pushed her out of the window you don't want her, so now she's mine.'

'I'll buy you another doll,' said Alicia frantically. 'We'll go to a toy shop—anywhere you like—and I'll buy you the best doll we can find. But give me back this one.'

'Shan't,' said the child.

Her arms went protectingly round the velvet doll.

'You *must* give her back,' said Sybil. 'She isn't yours.'

She stretched out to take the doll from the child and at that moment the child stamped her foot, turned, and screamed at them.

'Shan't! Shan't! Shan't! She's my very own. I love her. *You* don't love her. You hate her. If you didn't hate her you wouldn't have pushed her out of the window. I love her, I tell you, and that's what she wants. She *wants* to be loved.'

And then like an eel, sliding through the vehicles, the child ran across the street, down an alleyway, and out of sight before the two older women could decide to dodge the cars and follow.

'She's gone,' said Alicia.

'She said the doll wanted to be loved,' said Sybil.

'Perhaps,' said Alicia, 'perhaps that's what she wanted all along . . . to be loved . . .'

In the middle of the London traffic the two frightened women stared at each other.

In a Glass Darkly

I've no explanation of this story. I've no theories about the why and wherefore of it. It's just a thing—that happened.

All the same, I sometimes wonder how things would have gone if I'd noticed at the time just that one essential detail that I never appreciated until so many years afterwards. If I *had* noticed it—well, I suppose the course of three lives would have been entirely altered. Somehow—that's a very frightening thought.

For the beginning of it all, I've got to go back to the summer of 1914—just before the war—when I went down to Badgeworthy with Neil Carslake. Neil was, I suppose, about my best friend. I'd known his brother Alan too, but not so well. Sylvia, their sister, I'd never met. She was two years younger than Alan and three years younger than Neil. Twice, while we were at school together, I'd been going to spend part of the holidays with Neil at Badgeworthy and twice something had intervened. So it came about that I was twenty-three when I first saw Neil and Alan's home.

We were to be quite a big party there. Neil's sister Sylvia

had just got engaged to a fellow called Charles Crawley. He was, so Neil said, a good deal older than she was, but a thoroughly decent chap and quite reasonably well-off.

We arrived, I remember, about seven o'clock in the evening. Everyone had gone to his room to dress for dinner. Neil took me to mine. Badgeworthy was an attractive, rambling old house. It had been added to freely in the last three centuries and was full of little steps up and down, and unexpected staircases. It was the sort of house in which it's not easy to find your way about. I remember Neil promised to come and fetch me on his way down to dinner. I was feeling a little shy at the prospect of meeting his people for the first time. I remember saying with a laugh that it was the kind of house one expected to meet ghosts in the passages, and he said carelessly that he believed the place was said to be haunted but that none of them had ever seen anything, and he didn't even know what form the ghost was supposed to take.

Then he hurried away and I set to work to dive into my suitcases for my evening clothes. The Carslakes weren't well-off; they clung on to their old home, but there were no menservants to unpack for you or valet you.

Well, I'd just got to the stage of tying my tie. I was standing in front of the glass. I could see my own face and shoulders and behind them the wall of the room—a plain stretch of wall just broken in the middle by a door—and just as I finally settled my tie I noticed that the door was opening.

I don't know why I didn't turn around—I think that would have been the natural thing to do; anyway, I didn't.

I just watched the door swing slowly open—and as it swung I saw into the room beyond.

It was a bedroom—a larger room than mine—with two bedsteads in it, and suddenly I caught my breath.

For at the foot of one of those beds was a girl and round her neck were a pair of man's hands and the man was slowly forcing her backwards and squeezing her throat as he did so, so that the girl was being slowly suffocated.

There wasn't the least possibility of a mistake. What I saw was perfectly clear. What was being done was murder.

I could see the girl's face clearly, her vivid golden hair, the agonized terror of her beautiful face, slowly suffusing with blood. Of the man I could see his back, his hands, and a scar that ran down the left side of his face towards his neck.

It's taken some time to tell, but in reality only a moment or two passed while I stared dumbfounded. Then I wheeled round to the rescue . . .

And on the wall behind me, the wall reflected in the glass, there was only a Victorian mahogany wardrobe. No door open—no scene of violence. I swung back to the mirror. The mirror reflected only the wardrobe . . .

I passed my hands across my eyes. Then I sprang across the room and tried to pull forward the wardrobe and at that moment Neil entered by the other door from the passage and asked me what the hell I was trying to do.

He must have thought me slightly barmy as I turned on him and demanded whether there was a door behind the wardrobe. He said, yes, there was a door, it led into the next room. I asked him who was occupying the next room and he said people called Oldam—a Major Oldam and his wife. I asked him then if Mrs Oldam had very fair hair and when he replied dryly that she was dark I began to realize that I was probably making a fool of myself. I pulled myself together, made some lame explanation and we went downstairs together. I told myself that I must have had some kind of hallucination—and felt generally rather ashamed and a bit of an ass.

And then—and then—Neil said, 'My sister Sylvia,' and I was looking into the lovely face of the girl I had just seen being suffocated to death . . . and I was introduced to her fiancé, a tall dark man *with a scar down the left side of his face.*

Well—that's that. I'd like you to think and say what you'd have done in my place. Here was the girl—the identical girl—and here was the man I'd seen throttling her—and they were to be married in about a month's time . . .

Had I—or had I not—had a prophetic vision of the future? Would Sylvia and her husband come down here to stay some time in the future, and be given that room (the best spare room) and would that scene I'd witnessed take place in grim reality?

What was I to do about it? *Could* I do anything? Would anyone—Neil—or the girl herself—would they believe me?

I turned the whole business over and over in my mind the week I was down there. To speak or not to speak? And almost at once another complication set in. You see, I fell in love with Sylvia Carslake the first moment I saw here . . . I wanted her more than anything on earth . . . And in a way that tied my hands.

And yet, if I didn't say anything, Sylvia would marry Charles Crawley and Crawley would kill her . . .

And so, the day before I left, I blurted it all out to her. I said I expect she'd think me touched in the intellect or something, but I swore solemnly that I'd seen the thing just as I told it to her and that I felt if she was determined to marry Crawley, I ought to tell her my strange experience.

She listened very quietly. There was something in her eyes I didn't understand. She wasn't angry at all. When I'd finished, she just thanked me gravely. I kept repeating like an idiot, 'I *did* see it. I really did see it,' and she said, 'I'm sure you did if you say so. I believe you.'

Well, the upshot was that I went off not knowing whether I'd done right or been a fool, and a week later Sylvia broke off her engagement to Charles Crawley.

After that the war happened, and there wasn't much leisure for thinking of anything else. Once or twice when I was on leave, I came across Sylvia, but as far as possible I avoided her.

I loved her and wanted her just as badly as ever, but I felt somehow that it wouldn't be playing the game. It was owing to me that she'd broken off her engagement to Crawley, and I kept saying to myself that I could only justify the action I had taken by making my attitude a purely disinterested one.

Then, in 1916, Neil was killed and it fell to me to tell Sylvia about his last moments. We couldn't remain on formal footing after that. Sylvia had adored Neil and he had been my best friend. She was sweet—adorably sweet in her grief. I just managed to hold my tongue and went out again praying that a bullet might end the whole miserable business. Life without Sylvia wasn't worth living.

But there was no bullet with my name on it. One nearly got me below the right ear and one was deflected by a cigarette case in my pocket, but I came through unscathed. Charles Crawley was killed in action at the beginning of 1918.

Somehow that made a difference. I came home in the autumn of 1918 just before the Armistice and I went straight to Sylvia and told her that I loved her. I hadn't much hope that she'd care for me straight away, and you could have knocked me down with a feather when she asked me why I hadn't told her sooner. I stammered out something about Crawley and she said, 'But why did you think I broke it off with him?' and then she told me that she'd fallen in love with me just as I'd done with her—from the very first minute.

I said I thought she'd broken off her engagement because of the story I told her and she laughed scornfully and said that if you loved a man you wouldn't be as cowardly as that, and we went over that old vision of mine again and agreed that it was queer, but nothing more.

Well, there's nothing much to tell for some time after that. Sylvia and I were married and we were very happy. But I realized, as soon as she was really mine, that I wasn't cut out for the best kind of husband. I loved Sylvia devotedly, but I was jealous, absurdly jealous of anyone she so much as smiled at. It amused her at first, I think she even rather liked it. It proved, at least, how devoted I was.

As for me, I realized quite fully and unmistakably that I was not only making a fool of myself, but that I was endangering all the peace and happiness of our life together. I knew, I say, but I couldn't change. Every time Sylvia got a letter she didn't show to me I wondered who it was from. If she laughed and talked with any man, I found myself getting sulky and watchful.

At first, as I say, Sylvia laughed at me. She thought it a huge joke. Then she didn't think the joke so funny. Finally she didn't think it a joke at all—

And slowly, she began to draw away from me. Not in any physical sense, but she withdrew her secret mind from me. I no longer knew what her thoughts were. She was kind—but sadly, as thought from a long distance.

Little by little I realized that she no longer loved me. Her love had died and it was I who had killed it . . .

The next step was inevitable, I found myself waiting for it—dreading it . . .

Then Derek Wainwright came into our lives. He had everything that I hadn't. He had brains and a witty tongue. He was good-looking, too, and—I'm forced to admit it—a thoroughly good chap. As soon as I saw him I said to myself, 'This is just the man for Sylvia . . .'

She fought against it. I know she struggled . . . but I gave her no help. I couldn't. I was entrenched in my gloomy, sullen reserve. I was suffering like hell—and I couldn't stretch out a finger to save myself. I didn't help her. I made things worse. I let loose at her one day—a string of savage, unwarranted abuse. I was nearly mad with jealousy and misery. The things I said were cruel and untrue and I knew while I was saying them how cruel and how untrue they were. And yet I took a savage pleasure in saying them . . .

I remember how Sylvia flushed and shrank . . .

I drove her to the edge of endurance.

I remember she said, 'This can't go on . . .'

When I came home that night the house was empty—empty. There was a note—quite in the traditional fashion.

In it she said that she was leaving me—for good. She was going down to Badgeworthy for a day or two. After that she was going to the one person who loved her and needed her. I was to take that as final.

I suppose that up to then I hadn't really believed my own suspicions. This confirmation in black and white of my worst fears sent me raving mad. I went down to Badgeworthy after her as fast as the car would take me.

She had just changed her frock for dinner, I remember, when I burst into the room. I can see her face—startled—beautiful—afraid.

I said, 'No one but me shall ever have you. No one.'

And I caught her throat in my hands and gripped it and bent her backwards.

And suddenly I saw our reflection in the mirror. Sylvia choking and myself strangling her, and the scar on my cheek where the bullet grazed it under the right ear.

No—I didn't kill her. That sudden revelation paralysed me and I loosened my grasp and let her slip on to the floor . . .

And then I broke down—and she comforted me . . . Yes, she comforted me.

I told her everything and she told me that by the phrase 'the one person who loved and needed her' she had meant her brother Alan . . . We saw into each other's hearts that night, and I don't think, from that moment, that we ever drifted away from each other again . . .

It's a sobering thought to go through life with—that, but for the grace of God and a mirror, one might be a murderer . . .

One thing did die that night—the devil of jealousy that had possessed me so long . . .

But I wonder sometimes—suppose I hadn't made that initial mistake—the scar on the *left* cheek—when really it was the *right*—reversed by the mirror . . . Should I have been so sure the man was Charles Crawley? Would I have warned Sylvia? Would she be married to me—or to him?

Or are the past and the future all one?

I'm a simple fellow—and I can't pretend to understand these things—but I saw what I saw—and because of what I saw, Sylvia and I are together in the old-fashioned words—till death do us part. And perhaps beyond . . .

Greenshaw's Folly

The two men rounded the corner of the shrubbery.

'Well, there you are,' said Raymond West. 'That's it.'

Horace Bindler took a deep, appreciative breath.

'But my dear,' he cried, 'how wonderful.' His voice rose in a high screech of æsthetic delight, then deepened in reverent awe. 'It's unbelievable. Out of this world! A period piece of the best.'

'I thought you'd like it,' said Raymond West, complacently.

'Like it? My dear—' Words failed Horace. He unbuckled the strap of his camera and got busy. 'This will be one of the gems of my collection,' he said happily. 'I do think, don't you, that it's rather amusing to have a collection of monstrosities? The idea came to me one night seven years ago in my bath. My last real gem was in the Campo Santo at Genoa, but I really think this beats it. What's it called?'

'I haven't the least idea,' said Raymond.

'I suppose it's got a name?'

'It must have. But the fact is that it's never referred to round here as anything but Greenshaw's Folly.'

'Greenshaw being the man who built it?'

'Yes. In eighteen-sixty or seventy or thereabouts. The local success story of the time. Barefoot boy who had risen to immense prosperity. Local opinion is divided as to why he built this house, whether it was sheer exuberance of wealth or whether it was done to impress his creditors. If the latter, it didn't impress them. He either went bankrupt or the next thing to it. Hence the name, Greenshaw's Folly.'

Horace's camera clicked. 'There,' he said in a satisfied voice. 'Remind me to show you No. 310 in my collection. A really incredible marble mantelpiece in the Italian manner.' He added, looking at the house, 'I can't conceive of how Mr Greenshaw thought of it all.'

'Rather obvious in some ways,' said Raymond. 'He had visited the châteaux of the Loire, don't you think? Those turrets. And then, rather unfortunately, he seems to have travelled in the Orient. The influence of the Taj Mahal is unmistakable. I rather like the Moorish wing,' he added, 'and the traces of a Venetian palace.'

'One wonders how he ever got hold of an architect to carry out these ideas.'

Raymond shrugged his shoulders.

'No difficulty about that, I expect,' he said. 'Probably the architect retired with a good income for life while poor old Greenshaw went bankrupt.'

'Could we look at it from the other side?' asked Horace, 'or are we trespassing!'

'We're trespassing all right,' said Raymond, 'but I don't think it will matter.'

He turned towards the corner of the house and Horace skipped after him.

'But who lives here, my dear? Orphans or holiday visitors? It can't be a school. No playing-fields or brisk efficiency.'

'Oh, a Greenshaw lives here still,' said Raymond over his shoulder. 'The house itself didn't go in the crash. Old Greenshaw's son inherited it. He was a bit of a miser and lived here in a corner of it. Never spent a penny. Probably never had a penny to spend. His daughter lives here now. Old lady—very eccentric.'

As he spoke Raymond was congratulating himself on having thought of Greenshaw's Folly as a means of entertaining his guest. These literary critics always professed themselves as longing for a week-end in the country, and were wont to find the country extremely boring when they got there. Tomorrow there would be the Sunday papers, and for today Raymond West congratulated himself on suggesting a visit to Greenshaw's Folly to enrich Horace Bindler's well-known collection of monstrosities.

They turned the corner of the house and came out on a neglected lawn. In one corner of it was a large artificial rockery, and bending over it was a figure at sight of which Horace clutched Raymond delightedly by the arm.

'My dear,' he exclaimed, 'do you see what she's got on? A sprigged print dress. Just like a housemaid—when there were housemaids. One of my most cherished memories is staying at a house in the country when I was quite a boy where a real housemaid called you in the morning, all crackling in a print dress and a cap. Yes, my boy, really—a cap. Muslin with streamers. No, perhaps it was the parlour-maid who had the streamers. But anyway she was a real housemaid and she brought in an enormous brass can of hot water. What an exciting day we're having.'

The figure in the print dress had straightened up and had turned towards them, trowel in hand. She was a sufficiently startling figure. Unkempt locks of iron-grey fell wispily on her shoulders, a straw hat rather like the hats that horses wear in Italy was crammed down on her head. The coloured print dress she wore fell nearly to her ankles. Out of a weatherbeaten, not-too-clean face, shrewd eyes surveyed them appraisingly.

'I must apologize for trespassing, Miss Greenshaw,' said Raymond West, as he advanced towards her, 'but Mr Horace Bindler who is staying with me—'

Horace bowed and removed his hat.

'—is most interested in—er—ancient history and—er—fine buildings.'

Raymond West spoke with the ease of a well-known author who knows that he is a celebrity, that he can venture where other people may not.

Miss Greenshaw looked up at the sprawling exuberance behind her.

'It *is* a fine house,' she said appreciatively. 'My grandfather built it—before my time, of course. He is reported as having said that he wished to astonish the natives.'

'I'll say he did that, ma'am,' said Horace Bindler.

'Mr Bindler is the well-known literary critic,' said Raymond West.

Miss Greenshaw had clearly no reverence for literary critics. She remained unimpressed.

'I consider it,' said Miss Greenshaw, referring to the

house, 'as a monument to my grandfather's genius. Silly fools come here, and ask me why I don't sell it and go and live in a flat. What would *I* do in a flat? It's my home and I live in it,' said Miss Greenshaw. 'Always have lived here.' She considered, brooding over the past. 'There were three of us. Laura married the curate. Papa wouldn't give her any money, said clergymen ought to be unworldly. She died, having a baby. Baby died too. Nettie ran away with the riding master. Papa cut her out of his will, of course. Handsome fellow, Harry Fletcher, but no good. Don't think Nettie was happy with him. Anyway, she didn't live long. They had a son. He writes to me sometimes, but of course he isn't a Greenshaw. *I*'m the last of the Greenshaws.' She drew up her bent shoulders with a certain pride, and readjusted the rakish angle of the straw hat. Then, turning, she said sharply,

'Yes, Mrs Cresswell, what is it?'

Approaching them from the house was a figure that, seen side by side with Miss Greenshaw, seemed ludicrously dissimilar. Mrs Cresswell had a marvellously dressed head of well-blued hair towering upwards in meticulously arranged curls and rolls. It was as though she had dressed her head to go as a French marquise to a fancy-dressparty. The rest of her middle-aged person was dressed in what ought to have been rustling black silk but was actually one of the shinier varieties of black rayon. Although she was not a large woman, she had a well-developed and sumptuous bust. Her voice when she spoke, was unexpectedly deep. She spoke with exquisite diction, only a slight hesitation over words beginning with 'h' and the final pronunciation of them with an exaggerated aspirate gave rise to a suspicion that at some remote period in her youth she might have had trouble over dropping her h's.

'The fish, madam,' said Mrs Cresswell, 'the slice of cod. It has not arrived. I have asked Alfred to go down for it and he refuses to do so.'

Rather unexpectedly, Miss Greenshaw gave a cackle of laughter.

'Refuses, does he?'

'Alfred, madam, has been most disobliging.'

Miss Greenshaw raised two earth-stained fingers to her lips, suddenly produced an ear-splitting whistle and at the same time yelled:

'Alfred. Alfred, come here.'

Round the corner of the house a young man appeared in answer to the summons, carrying a spade in his hand. He had a bold, handsome face and as he drew near he cast an unmistakably malevolent glance towards Mrs Cresswell.

'You wanted me, miss?' he said.

'Yes, Alfred. I hear you've refused to go down for the fish. What about it, eh?'

Alfred spoke in a surly voice.

'I'll go down for it if you wants it, miss. You've only got to say.'

'I do want it. I want it for my supper.'

'Right you are, miss. I'll go right away.'

He threw an insolent glance at Mrs Cresswell, who flushed and murmured below her breath:

'Really! It's unsupportable.'

'Now that I think of it,' said Miss Greenshaw, 'a couple

of strange visitors are just what we need aren't they, Mrs Cresswell?'

Mrs Cresswell looked puzzled.

'I'm sorry, madam—'

'For you-know-what,' said Miss Greenshaw, nodding her head. 'Beneficiary to a will mustn't witness it. That's right, isn't it?' She appealed to Raymond West.

'Quite correct,' said Raymond.

'I know enough law to know that,' said Miss Greenshaw. 'And you two are men of standing.'

She flung down her trowel on her weeding-basket.

'Would you mind coming up to the library with me?'

'Delighted,' said Horace eagerly.

She led the way through french windows and through a vast yellow and gold drawing-room with faded brocade on the walls and dust covers arranged over the furniture, then through a large dim hall, up a staircase and into a room on the first floor.

'My grandfather's library,' she announced.

Horace looked round the room with acute pleasure. It was a room, from his point of view, quite full of monstrosities. The heads of sphinxes appeared on the most unlikely pieces of furniture, there was a colossal bronze representing, he thought, Paul and Virginia, and a vast bronze clock with classical motifs of which he longed to take a photograph.

'A fine lot of books,' said Miss Greenshaw.

Raymond was already looking at the books. From what he could see from a cursory glance there was no book here of any real interest or, indeed, any book which appeared to have been read. They were all superbly bound sets of the classics as supplied ninety years ago for furnishing a gentleman's library. Some novels of a bygone period were included. But they too showed little signs of having been read.

Miss Greenshaw was fumbling in the drawers of a vast desk. Finally she pulled out a parchment document.

'My will,' she explained. 'Got to leave your money to someone—or so they say. If I died without a will I suppose that son of a horse-coper would get it. Handsome fellow, Harry Fletcher, but a rogue if there ever was one. Don't see why *his* son should inherit this place. No,' she went on, as though answering some unspoken objection, 'I've made up my mind. I'm leaving it to Cresswell.'

'Your housekeeper?'

'Yes. I've explained it to her. I make a will leaving her all I've got and then I don't need to pay her any wages. Saves me a lot in current expenses, and it keeps her up to the mark. No giving me notice and walking off at any minute. Very la-di-dah and all that, isn't she? But her father was a working plumber in a very small way. *She*'s nothing to give herself airs about.'

She had by now unfolded the parchment. Picking up a pen she dipped it in the inkstand and wrote her signature, Katherine Dorothy Greenshaw.

'That's right,' she said. 'You've seen me sign it, and then you two sign it, and that makes it legal.'

She handed the pen to Raymond West. He hesitated a moment, feeling an unexpected repulsion to what he was asked to do. Then he quickly scrawled the well-known signature, for which his morning's mail usually brought at least six demands a day.

Horace took the pen from him and added his own minute signature.

'That's done,' said Miss Greenshaw.

She moved across to the bookcase and stood looking at them uncertainly, then she opened a glass door, took out a book and slipped the folded parchment inside.

'I've my own places for keeping things,' she said.

'*Lady Audley's Secret*,' Raymond West remarked, catching sight of the title as she replaced the book.

Miss Greenshaw gave another cackle of laughter.

'Best-seller in its day,' she remarked. 'Not like your books, eh?'

She gave Raymond a sudden friendly nudge in the ribs. Raymond was rather surprised that she even knew he wrote books. Although Raymond West was quite a name in literature, he could hardly be described as a best-seller. Though softening a little with the advent of middle-age, his books dealt bleakly with the sordid side of life.

'I wonder,' Horace demanded breathlessly, 'if I might just take a photograph of the clock?'

'By all means,' said Miss Greenshaw. 'It came, I believe, from the Paris exhibition.'

'Very probably,' said Horace. He took his picture.

'This room's not been used much since my grandfather's time,' said Miss Greenshaw. 'This desk's full of old diaries of his. Interesting, I should think. I haven't the eyesight to read them myself. I'd like to get them published, but I suppose one would have to work on them a good deal.'

'You could engage someone to do that,' said Raymond West.

'Could I really? It's an idea, you know. I'll think about it.'

Raymond West glanced at his watch.

'We mustn't trespass on your kindness any longer,' he said.

'Pleased to have seen you,' said Miss Greenshaw graciously. 'Thought you were the policeman when I heard you coming round the corner of the house.'

'Why a policeman?' demanded Horace, who never minded asking questions.

Miss Greenshaw responded unexpectedly.

'If you want to know the time, ask a policeman,' she carolled, and with this example of Victorian wit, nudged Horace in the ribs and roared with laughter.

'It's been a wonderful afternoon,' sighed Horace as they walked home. 'Really, that place has everything. The only thing the library needs is a body. Those old-fashioned detective stories about murder in the library—that's just the kind of library I'm sure the authors had in mind.'

'If you want to discuss murder,' said Raymond, 'you must talk to my Aunt Jane.'

'Your Aunt Jane? Do you mean Miss Marple?' He felt a little at a loss.

The charming old-world lady to whom he had been introduced the night before seemed the last person to be mentioned in connection with murder.

'Oh, yes,' said Raymond. 'Murder is a speciality of hers.'

'But my dear, how intriguing. What do you really mean?'

'I mean just that,' said Raymond. He paraphrased: 'Some commit murder, some get mixed up in murders, others have murder thrust upon them. My Aunt Jane comes into the third category.'

'You are joking.'

'Not in the least. I can refer you to the former Commissioner of Scotland Yard, several Chief Constables and one or two hard-working inspectors of the CID.'

Horace said happily that wonders would never cease. Over the tea table they gave Joan West, Raymond's wife, Lou Oxley her niece, and old Miss Marple, a résumé of the afternoon's happenings, recounting in detail everything that Miss Greenshaw had said to them.

'But I do think,' said Horace, 'that there is something a little *sinister* about the whole set-up. That duchess-like creature, the housekeeper—arsenic, perhaps, in the teapot, now that she knows her mistress has made the will in her favour?'

'Tell us, Aunt Jane,' said Raymond. 'Will there be murder or won't there? What do *you* think?'

'I think,' said Miss Marple, winding up her wool with a rather severe air, 'that you shouldn't joke about these things as much as you do, Raymond. Arsenic is, of course, *quite* a possibility. So easy to obtain. Probably present in the toolshed already in the form of weed killer.'

'Oh, really, darling,' said Joan West, affectionately. 'Wouldn't that be rather too obvious?'

'It's all very well to make a will,' said Raymond, 'I don't suppose really the poor old thing has anything to leave except that awful white elephant of a house, and who would want that?'

'A film company possibly,' said Horace, 'or a hotel or an institution?'

'They'd expect to buy it for a song,' said Raymond, but Miss Marple was shaking her head.

'You know, dear Raymond, I cannot agree with you there. About the money, I mean. The grandfather was evidently one of those lavish spenders who make money easily, but can't keep it. He may have gone broke, as you say, but hardly bankrupt or else his son would not have had the house. Now the son, as is so often the case, was an entirely different character to his father. A miser. A man who saved every penny. I should say that in the course of his lifetime he probably put by a very good sum. This Miss Greenshaw appears to have taken after him, to dislike spending money, that is. Yes, I should think it quite likely that she had quite a good sum tucked away.'

'In that case,' said Joan West, 'I wonder now—what about Lou?'

They looked at Lou as she sat, silent, by the fire.

Lou was Joan West's niece. Her marriage had recently, as she herself put it, come unstuck, leaving her with two young children and a bare sufficiency of money to keep them on.

'I mean,' said Joan, 'if this Miss Greenshaw really wants someone to go through diaries and get a book ready for publication . . .'

'It's an idea,' said Raymond.

Lou said in a low voice:

'It's work I could do—and I'd enjoy it.'

'I'll write to her,' said Raymond.

'I wonder,' said Miss Marple thoughtfully, 'what the old lady meant by that remark about a policeman?'

'Oh, it was just a joke.'

'It reminded me,' said Miss Marple, nodding her head vigorously, 'yes, it reminded me very much of Mr Naysmith.'

'Who was Mr Naysmith?' asked Raymond, curiously.

'He kept bees,' said Miss Marple, 'and was very good at doing the acrostics in the Sunday papers. And he liked giving people false impressions just for fun. But sometimes it led to trouble.'

Everybody was silent for a moment, considering Mr Naysmith, but as there did not seem to be any points of resemblance between him and Miss Greenshaw, they decided that dear Aunt Jane was perhaps getting a *little* bit disconnected in her old age.

Horace Bindler went back to London without having collected any more monstrosities and Raymond West wrote a letter to Miss Greenshaw telling her that he knew of a Mrs Louisa Oxley who would be competent to undertake work on the diaries. After a lapse of some days, a letter arrived, written in spidery old-fashioned handwriting, in which Miss Greenshaw declared herself anxious to avail herself of the services of Mrs Oxley, and making an appointment for Mrs Oxley to come and see her.

Lou duly kept the appointment, generous terms were arranged and she started work on the following day.

'I'm awfully grateful to you,' she said to Raymond. 'It will fit in beautifully. I can take the children to school, go on to Greenshaw's Folly and pick them up on my way back. How fantastic the whole set-up is! That old woman has to be seen to be believed.'

On the evening of her first day at work she returned and described her day.

'I've hardly seen the housekeeper,' she said. 'She came in with coffee and biscuits at half past eleven with her mouth pursed up very prunes and prisms, and would hardly speak to me. I think she disapproves deeply of my having been engaged.' She went on, 'It seems there's quite a feud between her and the gardener, Alfred. He's a local boy and fairly lazy, I should imagine, and he and the housekeeper won't speak to each other. Miss Greenshaw said in her rather grand way, "There have always been feuds as far as I can remember between the garden and the house staff. It was so in my grandfather's time. There were three men and a boy in the garden then, and eight maids in the house, but there was always friction."'

On the following day Lou returned with another piece of news.

'Just fancy,' she said, 'I was asked to ring up the nephew this morning.'

'Miss Greenshaw's nephew?'

'Yes. It seems he's an actor playing in the company that's doing a summer season at Boreham on Sea. I rang up the theatre and left a message asking him to lunch tomorrow. Rather fun, really. The old girl didn't want the housekeeper to know. I think Mrs Cresswell has done something that's annoyed her.'

'Tomorrow another instalment of this thrilling serial,' murmured Raymond.

'It's exactly like a serial, isn't it? Reconciliation with the nephew, blood is thicker than water—another will to be made and the old will destroyed.'

'Aunt Jane, you're looking very serious.'

'Was I, my dear? Have you heard any more about the policeman?'

Lou looked bewildered. 'I don't know anything about a policeman.'

'That remark of hers, my dear,' said Miss Marple, 'must have meant *something*.'

Lou arrived at her work the next day in a cheerful mood. She passed through the open front door—the doors and windows of the house were always open. Miss Greenshaw appeared to have no fear of burglars, and was probably justified, as most things in the house weighed several tons and were of no marketable value.

Lou had passed Alfred in the drive. When she first caught sight of him he had been leaning against a tree smoking a cigarette, but as soon as he had caught sight of her he had seized a broom and begun diligently to sweep leaves. An idle young man, she thought, but good looking. His features reminded her of someone. As she passed through the hall on her way upstairs to the library she glanced at the large picture of Nathaniel Greenshaw which presided over the mantelpiece, showing him in the acme of Victorian prosperity, leaning back in a large arm-chair, his hands resting on the gold albert across his capacious stomach. As her glance swept up from the stomach to the face with its heavy jowls, its bushy eyebrows and its flourishing black moustache, the thought occurred to her that Nathaniel Greenshaw must have been handsome as a young man. He had looked, perhaps, a little like Alfred . . .

She went into the library, shut the door behind her, opened her typewriter and got out the diaries from the drawer at the side of the desk. Through the open window she caught a glimpse of Miss Greenshaw in a puce-coloured sprigged print, bending over the rockery, weeding assiduously. They had had two wet days, of which the weeds had taken full advantage.

Lou, a town-bred girl, decided that if she ever had a garden it would never contain a rockery which needed hand weeding. Then she settled down to her work.

When Mrs Cresswell entered the library with the coffee tray at half past eleven, she was clearly in a very bad temper. She banged the tray down on the table, and observed to the universe:

'Company for lunch—and nothing in the house! What am *I* supposed to do, I should like to know? And no sign of Alfred.'

'He was sweeping in the drive when I got here,' Lou offered.

'I dare say. A nice soft job.'

Mrs Cresswell swept out of the room and banged the door behind her. Lou grinned to herself. She wondered what 'the nephew' would be like.

She finished her coffee and settled down to her work again. It was so absorbing that time passed quickly. Nathaniel Greenshaw, when he started to keep a diary, had succumbed to the pleasure of frankness. Trying out a passage relating to the personal charm of a barmaid in the neighbouring town, Lou reflected that a good deal of editing would be necessary.

As she was thinking this, she was startled by a scream from the garden. Jumping up, she ran to the open window. Miss Greenshaw was staggering away from the rockery towards the house. Her hands were clasped to her breast and between them there protruded a feathered shaft that Lou recognized with stupefaction to be the shaft of an arrow.

Miss Greenshaw's head, in its battered straw hat, fell forward on her breast. She called up to Lou in a failing voice: '. . . shot . . . he shot me . . . with an arrow . . . get help . . .'

Lou rushed to the door. She turned the handle, but the door would not open. It took her a moment or two of futile endeavour to realize that she was locked in. She rushed back to the window.

'I'm locked in.'

Miss Greenshaw, her back towards Lou, and swaying a little on her feet was calling up to the housekeeper at a window farther along.

'Ring police . . . telephone . . .'

Then, lurching from side to side like a drunkard she disappeared from Lou's view through the window below into the drawing-room. A moment later Lou heard a crash of broken china, a heavy fall, and then silence. Her imagination reconstructed the scene. Miss Greenshaw must have staggered blindly into a small table with a Sèvres teaset on it.

Desperately Lou pounded on the door, calling and shouting. There was no creeper or drain-pipe outside the window that could help her to get out that way.

Tired at last of beating on the door, she returned to the window. From the window of her sitting-room farther along, the housekeeper's head appeared.

'Come and let me out, Mrs Oxley. I'm locked in.'

'So am I.'

'Oh dear, isn't it awful? I've telephoned the police. There's an extension in this room, but what I can't understand, Mrs Oxley, is our being locked in. *I* never heard a key turn, did you?'

'No. I didn't hear anything at all. Oh dear, what shall we do? Perhaps Alfred might hear us.' Lou shouted at the top of her voice, 'Alfred, Alfred.'

'Gone to his dinner as likely as not. What time is it?'

Lou glanced at her watch.

'Twenty-five past twelve.'

'He's not supposed to go until half past, but he sneaks off earlier whenever he can.'

'Do you think—do you think—'

Lou meant to ask 'Do you think she's dead?' but the words stuck in her throat.

There was nothing to do but wait. She sat down on the window-sill. It seemed an eternity before the stolid helmeted figure of a police constable came round the corner of the house. She leant out of the window and he looked up at her, shading his eyes with his hand. When he spoke his voice held reproof.

'What's going on here?' he asked disapprovingly.

From their respective windows, Lou and Mrs Cresswell poured a flood of excited information down on him.

The constable produced a note-book and pencil. 'You

ladies ran upstairs and locked yourselves in? Can I have your names, please?'

'No. Somebody else locked us in. Come and let us out.'

The constable said reprovingly, 'All in good time,' and disappeared through the window below.

Once again time seemed infinite. Lou heard the sound of a car arriving, and, after what seemed an hour, but was actually three minutes, first Mrs Cresswell and then Lou, were released by a police sergeant more alert than the original constable.

'Miss Greenshaw?' Lou's voice faltered. 'What—what's happened?'

The sergeant cleared his throat.

'I'm sorry to have to tell you, madam,' he said, 'what I've already told Mrs Cresswell here. Miss Greenshaw is dead.'

'Murdered,' said Mrs Cresswell. 'That's what it is—murder.'

The sergeant said dubiously:

'Could have been an accident—some country lads shooting with bows and arrows.'

Again there was the sound of a car arriving. The sergeant said:

'That'll be the MO,' and started downstairs.

But it was not the MO. As Lou and Mrs Cresswell came down the stairs a young man stepped hesitatingly through the front door and paused, looking round him with a somewhat bewildered air.

Then, speaking in a pleasant voice that in some way seemed familiar to Lou—perhaps it had a family resemblance to Miss Greenshaw's—he asked:

'Excuse me, does—er—does Miss Greenshaw live here?'

'May I have your name if you please,' said the sergeant advancing upon him.

'Fletcher,' said the young man. 'Nat Fletcher. I'm Miss Greenshaw's nephew, as a matter of fact.'

'Indeed, sir, well—I'm sorry—I'm sure—'

'Has anything happened?' asked Nat Fletcher.

'There's been an—accident—your aunt was shot with an arrow—penetrated the jugular vein—'

Mrs Cresswell spoke hysterically and without her usual refinement:

'Your h'aunt's been murdered, that's what's 'appened. Your h'aunt's been murdered.'

Inspector Welch drew his chair a little nearer to the table and let his gaze wander from one to the other of the four people in the room. It was the evening of the same day. He had called at the Wests' house to take Lou Oxley once more over her statement.

'You are sure of the exact words? *Shot—he shot me—with an arrow—get help?*'

Lou nodded.

'And the time?'

'I looked at my watch a minute or two later—it was then twelve twenty-five.'

'Your watch keeps good time?'

'I looked at the clock as well.'

The inspector turned to Raymond West.

'It appears, sir, that about a week ago you and a

Mr Horace Bindler were witnesses to Miss Greenshaw's will?'

Briefly, Raymond recounted the events of the afternoon visit that he and Horace Bindler had paid to Greenshaw's Folly.

'This testimony of yours may be important,' said Welch. 'Miss Greenshaw distinctly told you, did she, that her will was being made in favour of Mrs Cresswell, the housekeeper, that she was not paying Mrs Cresswell any wages in view of the expectations Mrs Cresswell had of profiting by her death?'

'That is what she told me—yes.'

'Would you say that Mrs Cresswell was definitely aware of these facts?'

'I should say undoubtedly. Miss Greenshaw made a reference in my presence to beneficiaries not being able to witness a will and Mrs Cresswell clearly understood what she meant by it. Moreover, Miss Greenshaw herself told me that she had come to this arrangement with Mrs Cresswell.'

'So Mrs Cresswell had reason to believe she was an interested party. Motive's clear enough in her case, and I dare say she'd be our chief suspect now if it wasn't for the fact that she was securely locked in her room like Mrs Oxley here, and also that Miss Greenshaw definitely said a *man* shot her—'

'She definitely *was* locked in her room?'

'Oh yes. Sergeant Cayley let her out. It's a big old-fashioned lock with a big old-fashioned key. The key was in the lock and there's not a chance that it could have been turned from inside or any hanky-panky of that kind. No, you can take it definitely that Mrs Cresswell was locked inside that room and couldn't get out. And there were no bows and arrows in the room and Miss Greenshaw couldn't in any case have been shot from a window—the angle forbids it—no, Mrs Cresswell's out of it.'

He paused and went on:

'Would you say that Miss Greenshaw, in your opinion, was a practical joker?'

Miss Marple looked up sharply from her corner.

'So the will wasn't in Mrs Cresswell's favour after all?' she said.

Inspector Welch looked over at her in a rather surprised fashion.

'That's a very clever guess of yours, madam,' he said. 'No. Mrs Cresswell isn't named as beneficiary.'

'Just like Mr Naysmith,' said Miss Marple, nodding her head. 'Miss Greenshaw told Mrs Cresswell she was going to leave her everything and so got out of paying her wages; and then she left her money to somebody else. No doubt she was vastly pleased with herself. No wonder she chortled when she put the will away in *Lady Audley's Secret*.'

'It was lucky Mrs Oxley was able to tell us about the will and where it was put,' said the inspector. 'We might have had a long hunt for it otherwise.'

'A Victorian sense of humour,' murmured Raymond West.

'So she left her money to her nephew after all,' said Lou.

The inspector shook his head.

'No,' he said, 'she didn't leave it to Nat Fletcher. The story goes around here—of course I'm new to the place and I only get the gossip that's second-hand—but it seems that in the old days both Miss Greenshaw and her sister were set on the handsome young riding master, and the sister got him. No, she didn't leave the money to her nephew—' He paused, rubbing his chin, 'She left it to Alfred,' he said.

'Alfred—the gardener?' Joan spoke in a surprised voice.

'Yes, Mrs West. Alfred Pollock.'

'But why?' cried Lou.

Miss Marple coughed and murmured:

'I should imagine, though perhaps I am wrong, that there may have been—what we might call *family* reasons.'

'You could call them that in a way,' agreed the inspector. 'It's quite well known in the village, it seems, that Thomas Pollock, Alfred's grandfather, was one of old Mr Greenshaw's by-blows.'

'Of course,' cried Lou, 'the resemblance! I saw it this morning.'

She remembered how after passing Alfred she had come into the house and looked up at old Greenshaw's portrait.

'I dare say,' said Miss Marple, 'that she thought Alfred Pollock might have a pride in the house, might even want to live in it, whereas her nephew would almost certainly have no use for it whatever and would sell it as soon as he could possibly do so. He's an actor, isn't he? What play exactly is he acting in at present?'

Trust an old lady to wander from the point, thought Inspector Welch, but he replied civilly:

'I believe, madam, they are doing a season of James Barrie's plays.'

'Barrie,' said Miss Marple thoughtfully.

'*What Every Woman Knows*,' said Inspector Welch, and then blushed. 'Name of a play,' he said quickly. 'I'm not much of a theatre-goer myself,' he added, 'but the wife went along and saw it last week. Quite well done, she said it was.'

'Barrie wrote some very charming plays,' said Miss Marple, 'though I must say that when I went with an old friend of mine, General Easterly, to see Barrie's *Little Mary*—' she shook her head sadly, '—neither of us knew where to look.'

The inspector, unacquainted with the play *Little Mary*, looked completely fogged. Miss Marple explained:

'When I was a girl, Inspector, nobody ever mentioned the word *stomach*.'

The inspector looked even more at sea. Miss Marple was murmuring titles under her breath.

'*The Admirable Crichton*. Very clever. *Mary Rose*—a charming play. I cried, I remember. *Quality Street* I didn't care for so much. Then there was *A Kiss for Cinderella*. Oh, *of course*.'

Inspector Welch had no time to waste on theatrical discussion. He returned to the matter in hand.

'The question is,' he said, 'did Alfred Pollock know that the old lady had made a will in his favour? Did she tell him?' He added: 'You see—there's an archery club over at Boreham Lovell and *Alfred Pollock's a member*. He's a very good shot indeed with a bow and arrow.'

'Then isn't your case quite clear?' asked Raymond West. 'It would fit in with the doors being locked on the two women—he'd know just where they were in the house.'

The inspector looked at him. He spoke with deep melancholy.

'He's got an alibi,' said the inspector.

'I always think alibis are definitely suspicious.'

'Maybe, sir,' said Inspector Welch. 'You're talking as a writer.'

'I don't write detective stories,' said Raymond West, horrified at the mere idea.

'Easy enough to say that alibis are suspicious,' went on Inspector Welch, 'but unfortunately we've got to deal with facts.'

He sighed.

'We've got three good suspects,' he said. 'Three people who, as it happened, were very close upon the scene at the time. Yet the odd thing is that it looks as though none of the three could have done it. The housekeeper I've already dealt with—the nephew, Nat Fletcher, at the moment Miss Greenshaw was shot, was a couple of miles away filling up his car at a garage and asking his way—as for Alfred Pollock six people will swear that he entered the Dog and Duck at twenty past twelve and was there for an hour having his usual bread and cheese and beer.'

'Deliberately establishing an alibi,' said Raymond West hopefully.

'Maybe,' said Inspector Welch, 'but if so, he *did* establish it.'

There was a long silence. Then Raymond turned his head to where Miss Marple sat upright and thoughtful.

'It's up to you, Aunt Jane,' he said. 'The inspector's baffled, the sergeant's baffled, I'm baffled, Joan's baffled,

Lou is baffled. But to you, Aunt Jane, it is crystal clear. Am I right?'

'I wouldn't say that, dear,' said Miss Marple, 'not *crystal* clear, and murder, dear Raymond, isn't a game. I don't suppose poor Miss Greenshaw wanted to die, and it was a particularly brutal murder. Very well planned and quite cold blooded. It's not a thing to make *jokes* about!'

'I'm sorry,' said Raymond, abashed. 'I'm not really as callous as I sound. One treats a thing lightly to take away from the—well, the horror of it.'

'That is, I believe, the modern tendency,' said Miss Marple, 'All these wars, and having to joke about funerals. Yes, perhaps I was thoughtless when I said you were callous.'

'It isn't,' said Joan, 'as though we'd known her at all well.'

'That is *very* true,' said Miss Marple. 'You, dear Joan, did not know her at all. I did not know her at all. Raymond gathered an impression of her from one afternoon's conversation. Lou knew her for two days.'

'Come now, Aunt Jane,' said Raymond, 'tell us your views. You don't mind, Inspector?'

'Not at all,' said the inspector politely.

'Well, my dear, it would seem that we have three people who had, or might have thought they had, a motive to kill the old lady. And three quite simple reasons why none of the three could have done so. The housekeeper could not have done so because she was locked in her room and because Miss Greenshaw definitely stated that a *man* shot her. The gardener could not have done it because he was inside the Dog and Duck at the time the murder was committed, the nephew could not have done it because he was still some distance away in his car at the time of the murder.'

'Very clearly put, madam,' said the inspector.

'And since it seems most unlikely that any outsider should have done it, where, then, are we?'

'That's what the inspector wants to know,' said Raymond West.

'One so often looks at a thing the wrong way round,' said Miss Marple apologetically. 'If we can't alter the movements or the position of those three people, then couldn't we perhaps alter the time of the murder?'

'You mean that both my watch and the clock were wrong?' asked Lou.

'No dear,' said Miss Marple, 'I didn't mean that at all. I mean that the murder didn't occur when you thought it occurred.'

'But I *saw* it,' cried Lou.

'Well, what I have been wondering, my dear, was whether you weren't *meant* to see it. I've been asking myself, you know, whether that wasn't the real reason why you were engaged for this job.'

'What *do* you mean, Aunt Jane?'

'Well, dear, it seems odd. Miss Greenshaw did not like spending money, and yet she engaged you and agreed quite willingly to the terms you asked. It seems to me that perhaps you were meant to be there in that library on the first floor, looking out of the window so that you could be the key witness—someone from outside of irreproachable good faith—to fix a definite time and place for the murder.'

'But you can't mean,' said Lou, incredulously, 'that Miss Greenshaw *intended* to be murdered.'

'What I mean, dear,' said Miss Marple, 'is that you didn't really know Miss Greenshaw. There's no real reason, is there, why the Miss Greenshaw you saw when you went up to the house should be the same Miss Greenshaw that Raymond saw a few days earlier? Oh, yes, I know,' she went on, to prevent Lou's reply, 'she was wearing the peculiar old-fashioned print dress and the strange straw hat, and had unkempt hair. She corresponded exactly to the description Raymond gave us last week-end. But those two women, you know, were much of an age and height and size. The housekeeper, I mean, and Miss Greenshaw.'

'But the housekeeper is fat!' Lou exclaimed. 'She's got an enormous bosom.'

Miss Marple coughed.

'But my dear, surely, nowadays I have seen—er—them myself in shops most indelicately displayed. It is very easy for anyone to have a—a bust—of *any* size and dimension.'

'What are you trying to say?' demanded Raymond.

'I was just thinking, dear, that during the two or three days Lou was working there, one woman could have played the two parts. You said yourself, Lou, that you hardly saw the housekeeper, except for the one moment in the morning when she brought you in the tray with coffee. One sees those clever artists on the stage coming in as different characters with only a minute or two to spare, and I am sure the change could have been effected quite easily. That marquise head-dress could be just a wig slipped on and off.'

'Aunt Jane! Do you mean that Miss Greenshaw was dead before I started work there?'

'Not dead. Kept under drugs, I should say. A very easy job for an unscrupulous woman like the housekeeper to do. Then she made the arrangements with you and got you to telephone to the nephew to ask him to lunch at a definite time. The only person who would have known that this Miss Greenshaw was *not* Miss Greenshaw would have been Alfred. And if you remember, the first two days you were working there it was wet, and Miss Greenshaw stayed in the house. Alfred never came into the house because of his feud with the housekeeper. And on the last morning Alfred was in the drive, while Miss Greenshaw was working on the rockery—I'd like to have a look at that rockery.'

'Do you mean it was Mrs Cresswell who killed Miss Greenshaw?'

'I think that after bringing you your coffee, the woman locked the door on you as she went out, carried the unconscious Miss Greenshaw down to the drawing-room, then assumed her "Miss Greenshaw" disguise and went out to work on the rockery where you could see her from the window. In due course she screamed and came staggering to the house clutching an arrow as though it had penetrated her throat. She called for help and was careful to say "*he* shot me" so as to remove suspicion from the housekeeper. She also called up to the housekeeper's window as though she saw her there. Then, once inside the drawing-room, she threw over a table with porcelain on it—and ran quickly upstairs, put on her marquise wig and was able a few moments later to lean her head out of the window and tell you that she, too, was locked in.'

'But she *was* locked in,' said Lou.

'I know. That is where the policeman comes in.'

'What policeman?'

'Exactly—what policeman? I wonder, Inspector, if you would mind telling me how and when *you* arrived on the scene?'

The inspector looked a little puzzled.

'At twelve twenty-nine we received a telephone call from Mrs Cresswell, housekeeper to Miss Greenshaw, stating that her mistress had been shot. Sergeant Cayley and myself went out there at once in a car and arrived at the house at twelve thirty-five. We found Miss Greenshaw dead and the two ladies locked in their rooms.'

'So, you see, my dear,' said Miss Marple to Lou. 'The police constable *you* saw wasn't a real police constable. You never thought of him again—one doesn't—one just accepts one more uniform as part of the law.'

'But who—why?'

'As to who—well, if they are playing *A Kiss for Cinderella*, a policeman is the principal character. Nat Fletcher would only have to help himself to the costume he wears on the stage. He'd ask his way at a garage being careful to call attention to the time—twelve twenty-five, then drive on quickly, leave his car round a corner, slip on his police uniform and do his "act".'

'But why?—why?'

'*Someone* had to lock the housekeeper's door on the outside, and someone had to drive the arrow through

Miss Greenshaw's throat. You can stab anyone with an arrow just as well as by shooting it—but it needs force.'

'You mean they were both in it?'

'Oh yes, I think so. Mother and son as likely as not.'

'But Miss Greenshaw's sister died long ago.'

'Yes, but I've no doubt Mr Fletcher married again. He sounds the sort of man who would, and I think it possible that the child died too, and that this so-called nephew was the second wife's child, and not really a relation at all. The woman got a post as housekeeper and spied out the land. Then he wrote as her nephew and proposed to call upon her—he may have made some joking reference to coming in his policeman's uniform—or asked her over to see the play. But I think she suspected the truth and refused to see him. He would have been her heir if she had died without making a will—but of course once she had made a will in the housekeeper's favour (as they thought) then it was clear sailing.'

'But why use an arrow?' objected Joan. 'So very far fetched.'

'Not far fetched at all, dear. Alfred belonged to an archery club—Alfred was meant to take the blame. The fact that he was in the pub as early as twelve twenty was most unfortunate from their point of view. He always left a little before his proper time and that would have been just right—' she shook her head. 'It really seems all wrong—morally, I mean, that Alfred's laziness should have saved his life.'

The inspector cleared his throat.

'Well, madam, these suggestions of yours are very interesting. I shall have, of course, to investigate—'

*

Miss Marple and Raymond West stood by the rockery and looked down at that gardening basket full of dying vegetation.

Miss Marple murmured:

'Alyssum, saxifrage, cytisus, thimble campanula . . . Yes, that's all the proof *I* need. Whoever was weeding here yesterday morning was no gardener—she pulled up plants as well as weeds. So now I *know* I'm right. Thank you, dear Raymond, for bringing me here. I wanted to see the place for myself.'

She and Raymond both looked up at the outrageous pile of Greenshaw's Folly.

A cough made them turn. A handsome young man was also looking at the house.

'Plaguey big place,' he said. 'Too big for nowadays—or so they say. I dunno about that. If I won a football pool and made a lot of money, that's the kind of house I'd like to build.'

He smiled bashfully at them.

'Reckon I can say so now—that there house was built by my great-grandfather,' said Alfred Pollock. 'And a fine house it is, for all they call it Greenshaw's Folly!'

www.ingramcontent.com/pod-product-compliance
Ingram Content Group UK Ltd.
Pitfield, Milton Keynes, MK11 3LW, UK
UKHW022357170625
459797UK00007B/144